T0114101

P. G. WODEHOUSE

Bertie Wooster Sees It Through

Scribner Paperback Fiction

Published by Simon & Schuster

New York   London   Toronto   Sydney

SCRIBNER PAPERBACK FICTION
Simon & Schuster, Inc.
Rockefeller Center
1230 Avenue of the Americas
New York, NY 10020

First Scribner Paperback Fiction edition 2000
SCRIBNER PAPERBACK FICTION and design are trademarks
of Macmillan Library Reference USA, Inc., used under license
by Simon & Schuster, the publisher of this work.

DESIGNED BY ERICH HOBBING

Manufactured in the United States of America

3 5 7 9 10 8 6 4 2

Library of Congress Cataloging-in-Publication Data
Wodehouse, P. G. (Pelham Grenville), 1881–1975.
Bertie Wooster sees it through / P. G. Wodehouse.
—1st Scribner Paperback ed.
p. cm.
1. Wooster, Bertie (Fictitious character)—Fiction. 2. Jeeves
(Fictitious character)—Fiction. 3. Single men—Fiction.
4. Butlers—Fiction. 5. England—Fiction. I. Title.
PR6045.O53 B4 2000
823'.912—dc21   00-041999

ISBN 0-7432-0361-5 (Pbk)

Published in Great Britain as *Jeeves and the Feudal Spirit*

Dedication

TO

PETER SCHWED

(Of the firm of Simon and Schuster)

DEAR PETE,

I have rather gone off dedications these last forty years or so. To hell with them about sums up my attitude. Today, when I write a book, it's just a book, with no trimmings.

It was not always so. Back at the turn of the century I and the rest of the boys would as soon have gone out without our spats as allowed a novel of ours to go out practically naked, as you might say. The dedication was the thing on which we spread ourselves. I once planned a book which was to consist entirely of dedications, but abandoned the idea because I could not think of a dedication for it.

We went in for variety in those days. When you opened a novel, you never knew what you were going to get. It might be the curt take-it-or-leave-it dedication:

the somewhat warmer

To My Friend

PERCY BROWN

or one of those cryptic dedications with a bit of poetry
shoved in underneath in italics, like

TO F.B.O.

> *Stark winds*
> *And sunset over the moors.*
> *Why?*
> *Whither?*
> *Whence?*
> *And the sound of distant drums . . .*

J. FRED MUGGS

Lower-Smattering-on-the-Wissel, 1912

or possibly, if we were feeling a bit livery, the nasty dedication:

TO THE CRITICS

THESE PEARLS

It was all great fun and kept our pores open and
brought the roses to our cheeks, but most authors have
given it up. Inevitably a time came when there crept into
their minds the question "What is there in this for me?" I
know it was so in my case. "What is Wodehouse getting

out of this?" I asked myself, and the answer, as far as I could see, was, "Not a ruddy thing."

When the eighteenth-century writer inserted on Page One something like

To

THE MOST NOBLE AND PUISSANT

LORD KNUBBLE OF KNOPP

From

HIS VERY HUMBLE SERVANT

THE AUTHOR

My Lord.
It is with inexpressible admiration for your lordship's transcendent gifts that the poor slob who now addresses your lordship presents to your lordship this trifling work, so unworthy of your lordship's distinguished consideration

he expected to clean up. Lord Knubble was his patron and could be relied on, if given the old oil in liberal doses, to come through with at least a couple of guineas. But where does the modern author get off? He plucks—let us say—P. B. Biffen from the unsung millions and makes him immortal, and what does Biffen do in return? He does nothing. He just stands there. If he is like all the Biffens I know, the author won't get so much as a lunch out of it.

Nevertheless, partly because I know I shall get a very good lunch out of you but principally because you told Jack Goodman that you thought *Bertie Wooster Sees It Through* was better than *War and Peace* I inscribe this book

TO P.S.

Half a league
Half a league
Half a league
Onward
With a hey-nonny-nonny
And a hot cha-cha

P. G. WODEHOUSE

Colney Hatch, 1954

BERTIE WOOSTER
SEES IT THROUGH

1

AS I SAT in the bath tub, soaping a meditative foot and singing, if I remember correctly, "Pale Hands I Loved Beside The Shalimar," it would be deceiving my public to say that I was feeling boomps-a-daisy. The evening that lay before me promised to be one of those sticky evenings, no good to man or beast. My Aunt Dahlia, writing from her country residence, Brinkley Court down in Worcestershire, had asked me as a personal favor to take some acquaintances of hers out to dinner, a couple of the name of Trotter.

They were, she said, creeps of the first water and would bore the pants off me, but it was imperative that they be given the old oil, because she was in the middle of a very tricky business deal with the male half of the sketch and at such times every little helps. "Don't fail me, my beautiful bountiful Bertie," her letter had concluded, on a note of poignant appeal.

Well, this Dahlia is my good and deserving aunt, not to be confused with Aunt Agatha, the one who kills rats with her teeth and devours her young, so when she says Don't fail me, I don't fail her. But, as I say, I was in no sense looking forward to the binge. The view I took of it was that the curse had come upon me.

It had done so, moreover, at a moment when I was already lowered spiritually by the fact that for the last couple of weeks or so Jeeves had been away on his summer holiday. Round about the beginning of July each year he downs tools, the slacker, and goes off to Bognor Regis for the shrimping, leaving me in much the same position as those poets one used to have to read at school who were always beefing about losing gazelles. For without this righthand man at his side Bertram Wooster becomes a mere shadow of his former self and in no condition to cope with any ruddy Trotters.

Brooding darkly on these Trotters, whoever they might be, I was starting to scour the left elbow and had switched to "Ah, Sweet Mystery of Life," when my reverie was interrupted by the sound of a soft footstep in the bedroom, and I sat up, alert and, as you might say, agog, the soap frozen in my grasp. If feet were stepping softly in my sleeping quarters, it could only mean, I felt, unless of course a burglar had happened to drop in, that the prop of the establishment had returned from his vacation, no doubt looking bronzed and fit.

A quiet cough told me that I had reasoned astutely, and I gave tongue.

"Is that you, Jeeves?"

"Yes, sir."

"Home again, what?"

"Yes, sir."

"Welcome to 3 A Berkeley Mansions, London W.1," I said, feeling like a shepherd when a strayed sheep comes trickling back to the fold. "Did you have a good time?"

"Most agreeable, thank you, sir."

"You must tell me all about it."

"Certainly, sir, at your convenience."

"I'll bet you hold me spellbound. What are you doing in there?"

"A letter has just arrived for you, sir. I was placing it on the dressing table. Will you be dining in, sir?"

"No, out, blast it. A blind date with some slabs of gorgonzola sponsored by Aunt Dahlia. So if you want to go to the club, carry on."

As I have mentioned elsewhere in these memoirs of mine, Jeeves belongs to a rather posh club for butlers and valets called the Junior Ganymede, situated somewhere in Curzon Street, and I knew that after his absence from the metropolis he would be all eagerness to buzz round there and hobnob with the boys, picking up the threads and all that sort of thing. When I've been away for a week or two, my first move is always to make a beeline for the Drones.

"I'll bet you get a rousing welcome from the members, with a hey-nonny-nonny and a hot-cha-cha," I said. "Did I hear you say something about there being a letter for me?"

"Yes, sir. It was delivered a moment ago by special messenger."

"Important, do you think?"

"One can only conjecture, sir."

"Better open it and read contents."

"Very good, sir."

There was a stage wait of about a minute and a half, during which, my moodiness now much lightened, I rendered "Roll Out The Barrel," "I Love a Lassie," and "Every Day I Bring Thee Violets," in the order named. In due season his voice filtered through the woodwork.

"The letter is of considerable length, sir. Perhaps if I were to give you its substance?"

"Do so, Jeeves. All ready at this end."

"It is from a Mr. Percy Gorringe, sir. Omitting extraneous matter and concentrating on essentials, Mr. Gorringe wishes to borrow a thousand pounds from you."

I started sharply, causing the soap to shoot from my hand and fall with a dull thud on the bath mat. With no preliminary warning to soften the shock, his words had momentarily unmanned me. It is not often that one is confronted with ear-biting on so majestic a scale, a fiver till next Wednesday being about the normal tariff.

"You said . . . *what*, Jeeves? A thousand pounds? But who is this hound of hell? I don't know any Gorringes."

"I gather from his communication that you and the gentleman have not met, sir. But he mentions that he is the stepson of a Mr. L. G. Trotter, with whom Mrs. Travers appears to be acquainted."

I nodded. Not much use, of course, as he couldn't see me.

"Yes, he's on solid ground there," I admitted. "Aunt Dahlia does know Trotter. He's the bloke she has asked me to put the nosebag on with tonight. So far, so good. But I don't see that being Trotter's stepson entitles this Gorringe to think he can sit on my lap and help himself to the contents of my wallet. I mean, it isn't a case of 'Any stepson of yours, L. G. Trotter, is a stepson of mine.' Dash it, Jeeves, once start letting yourself be touched by stepsons, and where are you? The word flies round the family circle that you're a good provider, and up roll all the sisters and cousins and aunts and nephews and uncles to stake out their claims, several being injured in the crush. The place becomes a shambles."

"There is much in what you say, sir, but it appears to be not so much a loan as an investment that the gentleman is seeking. He wishes to give you the opportunity of contributing the money to the production of his dramatization of Lady Florence Craye's novel *Spindrift*."

"Oh, that's it, is it? I see. Yes, one begins to follow the trend of thought."

This Florence Craye is . . . well, I suppose you would call her a sort of step-cousin of mine or cousin once removed or something of that nature. She is Lord Worplesdon's daughter, and old W. in a moment of temporary insanity recently married my Aunt Agatha *en secondes noces,* as I believe the expression is. She is one of those intellectual girls, her bean crammed to bursting point with the little gray cells, and about a year ago, possibly because she was full of the divine fire but more probably because she wanted something to take her mind off Aunt Agatha, she wrote this novel and it was well received by the intelligentsia, who notoriously enjoy the most frightful bilge.

"Did you ever read *Spindrift*?" I asked, retrieving the soap.

"I skimmed through it, sir."

"What did you think of it? Go on, Jeeves, don't be coy. The word begins with an l."

"Well, sir, I would not go so far as to apply to it the adjective which I fancy you have in mind, but it seemed to me a somewhat immature production, lacking in significant form. My personal tastes lie more in the direction of Dostoyevsky and the great Russians. Nevertheless, the story was not wholly devoid of interest and might quite possibly have its appeal for the theater-going public."

I mused awhile. I was trying to remember something, but couldn't think what. Then I got it.

"But I don't understand this," I said. "I distinctly recall Aunt Dahlia telling me that Florence had told her that some manager had taken the play and was going to put it on. Poor misguided sap, I recollect saying. Well, if that is so, why is Percy dashing about trying to get into people's ribs like this? What does he want a thousand quid for? These are deep waters, Jeeves."

"That is explained in the gentleman's letter, sir. It appears that one of the syndicate financing the venture, who had promised the sum in question, finds himself unable to fulfill his obligations. This, I believe, frequently happens in the world of the theater."

I mused again, letting the moisture from the sponge slide over the torso. Another point presented itself.

"But why didn't Florence tell Percy to go and have a pop at Stilton Cheesewright? She being engaged to him, I mean. One would have thought that Stilton, linked to her by bonds of love, would have been the people's choice."

"Possibly Mr. Cheesewright has not a thousand pounds at his disposal, sir."

"That's true. I see what you're driving at. Whereas I have, you mean?"

"Precisely, sir."

The situation had clarified somewhat. Now that I had the facts, I could discern that Percy's move had been based on sound principles. When you are trying to raise a thousand quid, the first essential, of course, is to go to someone who has got a thousand quid, and no doubt he had learned from Florence that I was stagnant with the stuff. But where he had made his error was in supposing that I was the king of the mugs and in the habit of scattering vast sums like birdseed to all and sundry.

"Would you back a play, Jeeves?"

"No, sir."

"Nor would I. I meet him with a firm nolle prosequi, I

think, don't you, and keep the money in the old oak chest?"

"I would certainly advocate such a move, sir."

"Right. Percy gets the bird. Let him eat cake. And now to a more urgent matter. While I'm dressing, will you be mixing me a strengthening cocktail?"

"Certainly, sir. A martini or one of my specials?"

"The latter."

I spoke in no uncertain voice. It was not merely the fact that I was up against an evening with a couple whom Aunt Dahlia, always a good judge, had described as creeps that influenced this decision on my part. I needed fortifying for another reason.

These last few days, with Jeeves apt to return at any moment, it had been borne in upon me quite a good deal that when the time came for us to stand face to face I should require something pretty authoritative in the way of bracers to nerve me for what would inevitably be a testing encounter, calling for all that I had of determination and the will to win. If I was to emerge from it triumphant, no stone must be left unturned and no avenue unexplored.

You know how it is when two strong men live in close juxtaposition, if juxtaposition is the word I want. Differences arise. Wills clash. Bones of contention pop up and start turning handsprings. No one was more keenly alive than I to the fact that one such bone was scheduled to make its debut the instant I swam into his ken, and mere martinis, I felt, despite their numerous merits, would not be enough to see me through the ordeal that confronted me.

It was in quite fairly tense mood that I dried and clothed the person, and while it would perhaps be too much to say that as I entered the sitting-room some quarter of an hour later I was a-twitter, I was unquestionably conscious of a certain jumpiness. When Jeeves came in with the shaker, I dived at it like a seal going after a slice of fish and drained a quick one, scarcely pausing to say "Skin off your nose."

The effect was magical. That apprehensive feeling left me, to be succeeded by a quiet sense of power. I cannot put it better than by saying that as the fire coursed through my veins, Wooster the timid fawn became in a flash Wooster the man of iron will, ready for anything. What Jeeves inserts in these specials of his I have never ascertained, but their morale-building force is extraordinary. They wake the sleeping tiger in a chap. Well, to give you some idea, I remember once after a single one of them striking the table with clenched fist and telling my Aunt Agatha to stop talking rot. And I'm not sure it wasn't "bally rot."

"One of your best and brightest, Jeeves," I said, refilling the glass. "The weeks among the shrimps have not robbed your hand of its cunning."

He did not reply. Speech seemed to have been wiped from his lips, and I saw, as I had foreseen would happen, that his gaze was riveted on the upper slopes of my mouth. It was a cold, disapproving gaze, such as a fastidious luncher who was not fond of caterpillars might have directed at one which he had discovered in his portion of salad, and I knew that the clash of wills for which I had been bracing myself was about to raise its ugly head.

I spoke suavely but firmly. You can't beat suave firmness on these occasions, and thanks to that life-giving special I was able to be as firmly suave as billy-o. There was no mirror in the sitting-room, but had there been and had I caught a glimpse of myself in it, I have no doubt I should have seen something closely resembling a haughty seigneur of the old regime about to tell the domestic staff just where it got off.

"Something appears to be arresting your attention, Jeeves. Is there a smut on my nose?"

His manner continued frosty. There are moments when he looks just like a governess, one of which was this one.

"No, sir. It is on the upper lip. A dark stain like mulligatawny soup."

I gave a careless nod.

"Ah, yes," I said. "The moustache. That is what you are alluding to, is it not? I grew it while you were away. Rather natty, don't you think?"

"No, sir, I do not."

I moistened my lips with the special, still suave to the gills. I felt strong and masterful.

"You dislike the little thing?"

"Yes, sir."

"You don't feel it gives me a sort of air? A . . . how shall I put it? . . . a kind of diablerie?"

"No, sir."

"You hurt and disappoint me, Jeeves," I said, sipping a couple of sips and getting suaver all the time. "I could understand your attitude if the object under advisement were something bushy and waxed at the ends like a sergeant major's, but it is merely the delicate wisp of vegetation with which David Niven has for years been winning the applause of millions. When you see David Niven on the screen, you don't recoil in horror, do you?"

"No, sir. His moustache is very becoming to Mr. Niven."

"But mine isn't to me?"

"No, sir."

It is at moments like this that a man realizes that the

only course for him to pursue, if he is to retain his self-respect, is to unship the velvet hand in the iron glove, or, rather, the other way about. Weakness at such a time is fatal.

There are limits, I mean to say, and sharply defined limits at that, and these limits I felt that he had passed by about a mile and a quarter. I yield to nobody in my respect for Jeeves's judgment in the matter of socks, shoes, shirts, hats, and cravats, but I was dashed if I was going to have him muscling in and trying to edit the Wooster face. I finished my special and spoke in a quiet, level voice.

"I am sorry, Jeeves. I had hoped for your sympathy and cooperation, but if you are unable to see your way to sympathizing and cooperating, so be it. Come what may, however, I shall maintain the status quo. It is status quos that people maintain, isn't it? I have been put to considerable trouble and anxiety growing this moustache, and I do not propose to hew it off just because certain prejudiced parties, whom I will not specify, don't know a good thing when they see one. *J'y suis, j'y reste*, Jeeves," I said, becoming a bit Parisian.

Well, after this splendid exhibition of resolution on my part I suppose there was nothing much the chap could have said except "Very good, sir" or something of that sort, but, as it happened, he hadn't time to say even that, for the final word had scarcely left my lips when the front door bell tootled. He shimmered out, and a moment later shimmered in again.

"Mr. Cheesewright," he announced.

And in clumped the massive form of the bird to whom he alluded. The last person I had expected to see, and, for the matter of that, about the last one I wanted to.

I DON'T KNOW if you have had the same experience, but I have always found that there are certain blokes whose mere presence tends to make me ill at ease, inducing the nervous laugh, the fiddling with the tie and the embarrassed shuffling of the feet. Sir Roderick Glossop, the eminent looney doctor, until circumstances so arranged themselves that I was enabled to pierce the forbidding exterior and see his better, softer side, was one of these. J. Washburn Stoker, with his habit of kidnaping people on his yacht and generally throwing his weight about like a pirate of the Spanish Main, was another. And a third is this G. D'Arcy (Stilton) Cheesewright. Catch Bertram Wooster *vis-à-vis* with him, and you do not catch him at his best.

Considering that he and I have known each other since, as you might say, we were so high, having been at private school, Eton and Oxford together, we ought, I suppose, to be like Damon and what's-his-name, but we aren't by any means. I generally refer to him in conversation as "that blighter Stilton," while he, I have been informed by usually reliable sources, makes no secret of his surprise and concern that I am still on the right side of the walls of Colney Hatch or some similar institution. When we meet, there is always a certain stiffness and what Jeeves would call an imperfect fusion of soul.

One of the reasons for this is, I think, that Stilton used to be a policeman. He joined the Force on coming down from Oxford with the idea of rising to a position of eminence at Scotland Yard, a thing you find a lot of the fellows you know doing these days. True, he turned in his truncheon and whistle shortly afterwards because his uncle wanted him to take up another walk in life, but these rozzers, even when retired, never quite shake off that "Where were you on the night of June the fifteenth?" manner, and he seldom fails, when we run into one another, to make me feel like a rat of the underworld detained for questioning in connection with some recent smash-and-grab raid.

Add the fact that this uncle of his wins his bread as a magistrate at one of the London police courts, and you will understand why I avoid him as much as possible and greatly prefer him elsewhere. The man of sensibility shrinks from being closeted with an ex-bluebottle with magistrate blood in him.

In my demeanor, accordingly, as I rose to greet him, a close observer would have noted more than a touch of that To-what-am-I-indebted-for-the-honor-of-this-visit stuff. I was at a loss to imagine what he was doing invading my privacy like this, and another thing that had me fogged was why, having invaded it, he was standing staring at me in a stern, censorious sort of way, as if the sight of me had got right in amongst him, revolting his finest feelings. I might have been some dreg of society whom he had caught in the act of slipping a couple of ounces of cocaine to some other dreg.

"Ho!" he said, and this alone would have been enough to tell an intelligent bystander, had there been one, that he had spent some time in the ranks of the Force. One of the first things the Big Four teach the young recruit is to say "Ho!" "I thought as much," he went on, knitting the brow. "Swilling cocktails, eh?"

This was the moment when, had conditions been normal, I would no doubt have laughed nervously, fingered the tie and shuffled the feet, but with two of Jeeves's specials under my belt, still exercising their powerful spell, I not only remained intrepid but retorted with considerable spirit, putting him right in his place.

"I fail to understand you, officer," I said coldly. "Correct me if I am wrong, but I believe this is the hour when it is customary for an English gentleman to partake of a short snifter. Will you join me?"

His lip curled. Most unpleasant. These coppers are bad enough when they leave their lips in statu quo.

"No, I won't," he replied, curtly and offensively. "*I* don't want to ruin my constitution. What do you suppose those things are going to do to your eye and your power of control? How can you expect to throw doubles if you persist in stupefying yourself with strong drink? It's heartbreaking."

I saw all. He was thinking of the Darts sweep.

The annual Darts sweep is one of the high spots of life at the Drones Club. It never fails to stir the sporting instincts of the members, causing them to roll up in dense crowds and purchase tickets at ten bob a go, with the result that the sum in the kitty is always colossal. This time my name had been drawn by Stilton, and as Horace Pendlebury-Davenport, last year's winner, had gone and got married and at his wife's suggestion resigned his membership, the thing was pretty generally recognized as a sitter for me, last year's runner-up. "Wooster," the word flew to and fro, "is the deadest of snips. He throws a beautiful dart."

So I suppose it was only natural in a way that, standing, if all went well, to scoop in a matter of fifty-six pounds ten shillings, Stilton should feel that it was his mission in life to see that I kept at the peak of my form. But that didn't make this incessant surveillance of his easier to endure. Ever since he had glanced at his ticket, seen that it bore the name Wooster, and learned that I was a red-hot favorite for the tourney, his attitude towards me had been that of an official at Borstal told off to keep an eye on a more than ordinarily up-and-coming juvenile delinquent. He had a way of looming up beside me at the club, sniffing quickly at my glass and giving me an accusing look, coupled with a sharp whistling intake of the breath, and here he was now doing the same thing in my very home. It was worse than being back in a Little Lord Fauntleroy suit and ringlets and having a keen-eyed nurse always at one's elbow, watching one's every move like a bally hawk.

I was about to say how deeply I resented being tailed up in this manner, when he resumed.

"I have come here tonight to talk seriously to you, Wooster," he said, frowning in a most unpleasant manner. "I am shocked at the casual, frivolous way in which you are treating this Darts tournament. You seem not to be taking the most elementary precautions to ensure victory on the big day. It's the old, old story. Overconfidence. All these fatheads keep telling you you're sure to win, and you suck it down like one of your beastly cocktails. Well, let me tell you you're living in a fool's Paradise. I happened to look in at the Drones this afternoon, and Freddie Widgeon was at the Darts board, stunning all beholders with a performance that took the breath away. His accuracy was sensational."

I waved a hand and tossed the head. In fact, I suppose you might say I bridled. He had wounded my *amour propre.*

"Tchah!" I said, registering scorn.

"Eh?"

"I said 'Tchah!' With ref. to F. Widgeon. I know his form backwards. Flashy, but no staying power. The man will be less than the dust beneath my chariot wheels."

"That's what you think. As I said before, overconfidence. You can take it from me that Freddie is a very dangerous competitor. I happen to know that he has been in strict training for weeks. He's knocked off smoking and has a cold bath every morning. Did you have a cold bath this morning?"

"Certainly not. What do you suppose the hot tap's for?"

"Do you do Swedish exercises before breakfast?"

"I wouldn't dream of such a thing. Leave these excesses to the Swedes, I say."

"No," said Stilton bitterly. "All you do is riot and revel and carouse. I am told that you were at that party of Catsmeat Potter-Pirbright's last night. You probably reeled home at three in the morning, rousing the neighborhood with drunken shouts."

I raised a haughty eyebrow. This police persecution was intolerable. Was I in Russia?

"You would scarcely expect me, constable," I said coldly, "to absent myself from the farewell supper of a boyhood friend who is leaving for Hollywood in a day or two and may be away from civilization for years. Catsmeat would have been pained in his foundations if I had oiled out. And it wasn't three in the morning, it was two-thirty."

"Did you drink anything?"

"The merest sip."

"And smoke?"

"The merest cigar."

"I don't believe you. I'll bet, if the truth was known," said Stilton morosely, intensifying the darkness of his frown, "you lowered yourself to the level of the beasts of the field. I'll bet you whooped it up like a sailor in a Marseilles *bistro*. And from the fact that there is a white tie round your neck and a white waistcoat attached to your foul stomach at this moment I gather that you are planning to be off shortly to some other nameless orgy."

I laughed one of my quiet laughs. The word amused me.

"Orgy, eh? I'm giving dinner to some friends of my Aunt Dahlia's, and she strictly warned me to lay off the old Falernian because my guests are teetotalers. When the landlord fills the flowing bowl, it will be with lemonade, barley water, or possibly lime juices. So much for your nameless orgies."

This, as I had expected, had a mollifying effect on his acerbity, if acerbity is the word I want. He did not become genial, because he couldn't, but he became as nearly genial as it was in his power to be. He practically smiled.

"Capital," he said. "Capital. Most satisfactory."

"I'm glad you're pleased. Well, good night."

"Teetotalers, eh? Yes, that's excellent. But avoid all rich foods and sauces and be sure to get to bed early. What was that you said?"

"I said good night. You'll be wanting to run along, no doubt."

"I'm not running along." He looked at his watch. "Why the devil are women always late?" he said peevishly. "She ought to have been here long ago. I've told her over and over again that if there's one thing that makes Uncle Joe furious, it's being kept waiting for his soup."

This introduction of the sex motif puzzled me.

"She?"

"Florence. She is meeting me here. We're dining with my uncle."

"Oh, I see. Well, well. So Florence will be with us ere long, will she? Splendid, splendid, splendid."

I spoke with quite a bit of warmth and animation, trying to infuse a cheery note into the proceedings, and immediately wished I hadn't, because he quivered like a palsy patient and gave me a keen glance, and I saw that we had got on to dangerous ground. A situation of considerable delicacy had been precipitated.

One of the things which make it difficult to bring about a beautiful friendship between G. D'Arcy Cheesewright and self is the fact that not long ago I unfortunately got tangled up in his love life. Incensed by some crack he had made about modern enlightened thought, modern enlightened thought being practically a personal buddy of hers, Florence gave him the swift heave-ho and—much against my will, but she seemed to wish it—became betrothed to me. And this had led Stilton, a man of volcanic passions, to express a desire to tear me limb from limb and dance buck-and-wing dances on my remains. He also spoke of stirring up my face like an omelette and buttering me over the West End of London.

Fortunately before matters could proceed to this awful extreme love resumed work at the old stand, with the result that my nomination was canceled and the peril passed, but he has never really got over the distressing episode. Ever since then the green-eyed monster has always been more or less round and about, ready to snap into action at the drop of the hat, and he has tended to docket me as a snake in the grass that can do with a lot of watching.

So, though disturbed, I was not surprised that he now gave me that keen glance and spoke in a throaty growl, like a Bengal tiger snarling over its breakfast coolie.

"What do you mean, splendid? Are you so anxious to see her?"

I saw that tact would be required.

"Not anxious, exactly," I said smoothly. "The word is too strong. It's just that I would like to have her opinion of this moustache of mine. She is a girl of taste, and I would be prepared to accept the verdict. Shortly before you arrived, Jeeves was subjecting the growth to some destructive criticism, and it shook me a little. What do you think of it, by the way?"

"I think it's ghastly."

"Ghastly?"

"Revolting. You look like something in the chorus line of a touring revue. But you say Jeeves doesn't like it?"

"He didn't seem to."

"Ah, so you'll have to shave it. Thank God for that."

I stiffened. I resent the view, so widely held in my circle of acquaintance, that I am a mere Hey-you in the home, bowing to Jeeves's behests like a Hollywood yes-man.

"Over my dead body I'll shave it. It stays just where it is, rooted to the spot. A fig for Jeeves, if I may use the expression."

He shrugged his shoulders.

"Well, it's up to you, I suppose. If you don't mind making yourself an eyesore—"

I stiffened a bit further.

"Did you say eyesore?"

"Eyesore was what I said."

"Oh, it was, was it?" I riposted, and it is possible that, had we not been interrupted, the exchanges would have become heated, for I was still under the stimulating influence of those specials and in no mood to brook backchat. But before I could tell him that he was a fatheaded ass, incapable of recognizing the rare and the beautiful if handed to him on a skewer, the doorbell rang again and Jeeves announced Florence.

3

IT'S JUST OCCURRED TO ME, thinking back, that in that passage where I gave a brief pen portrait of her—fairly near the start of this narrative, if you remember—I may have made a bloomer and left you with a wrong impression of Florence Craye. Informed that she was an intellectual girl who wrote novels and was like ham and eggs with the boys with the bulging foreheads out Bloomsbury way, it is possible that you conjured up in your mind's eye the picture of something short and dumpy with ink spots on the chin, as worn by so many of the female intelligentsia.

Such is far from being the truth. She is tall and willowy and handsome, with a terrific profile and luxuriant platinum blonde hair, and might, so far as looks are concerned, be the star unit of the harem of one of the better class sultans. I have known strong men to be bowled over by her at first sight, and it is seldom that she takes her walks abroad without being whistled at by visiting Americans.

She came breezing in, dressed up to the nines, and Stilton received her with a cold eye on his wrist watch.

"So there you are at last," he said churlishly. "About time, dash it. I suppose you had forgotten that Uncle Joe has a nervous breakdown if he's kept waiting for his soup."

I was expecting some haughty response to this crack for I knew her to be a girl of spirit, but she ignored the rebuke, and I saw that her eyes, which are bright and hazel in color, were resting on me with a strange light in them. I don't know if you have ever seen a female of what they call teen-age gazing raptly at Humphrey Bogart in a cinema, but her deportment was much along those lines. More than a touch of the Soul's Awakening, if I make my meaning clear.

"Bertie!" she yipped, shaking from stem to stern. "The moustache! It's *lovely*! Why have you kept this from us all these years? It's wonderful. It gives you such a dashing look. It alters your whole appearance."

Well, after the bad press the old fungus had been getting of late, you might have thought that a rave notice like this would have been right up my street. I mean, while one lives for one's Art, so to speak, and cares little for the public's praise or blame and all that sort of thing, one can always do with something to paste into one's scrapbook, can one not? But it left me cold, particularly in the vicinity of the feet. I found my eye swiveling round to Stilton, to see how he was taking it, and was concerned to note that he was taking it extremely big.

Pique. That's the word I was trying to think of. He was looking definitely piqued, like a diner in a restaurant who has bitten into a bad oyster, and I wasn't sure I altogether blamed him, for his loved one had not only patted my cheek with an affectionate hand but was drinking me in with such wide-eyed admiration that any fiancé, witnessing the spectacle, might well have been excused for growing a bit hot under the collar. And Stilton, of course, as I have already indicated, was a chap who could give Othello a couple of bisques and be dormy one at the eighteenth.

It seemed to me that unless prompt steps were taken through the proper channels, raw passions might be unchained, so I hastened to change the subject.

"Tell me all about your uncle, Stilton," I said. "Fond of soup, is he? Quite a boy for the bouillon, yes?"

He merely gave a grunt like a pig dissatisfied with its ration for the day, so I changed the subject again.

"How is *Spindrift* going?" I asked Florence. "Still selling pretty copiously?"

I had said the right thing. She beamed.

"Yes, it's doing splendidly. It has just gone into another edition."

"That's good."

"You knew it had been made into a play?"

"Eh? Oh, yes. Yes, I heard about that."

"Do you know Percy Gorringe?"

I winced a trifle. Proposing, as I did, to expunge the joy from Percy's life by giving him the uncompromising miss-in-baulk before tomorrow's sun had set, I would have preferred to keep him out of the conversation. I said the name seemed somehow familiar, as if I had heard it somewhere in some connection.

"He did the dramatization. He has made a splendid job of it."

Here Stilton, who appeared to be allergic to Gorringes, snorted in his uncouth way. There are two things I particularly dislike about G. D'Arcy Cheesewright—one, his habit of saying "Ho!" the other his tendency, when moved, to make a sound like a buffalo pulling its foot out of a swamp.

"We have a manager who is going to put it on and he's got the cast and all that, but there has been an unfortunate hitch."

"You don't say?"

"Yes. One of the backers has failed us, and we need another thousand pounds. Still, it's going to be all right. Percy assures me he can raise the money."

Again I winced, and once more Stilton snorted. It is always difficult to weigh snorts in the balance, but I think this second one had it over the first in offensiveness by a small margin.

"That louse?" he said. "He couldn't raise tuppence."

These, of course, were fighting words. Florence's eyes flashed.

"I won't have you calling Percy a louse. He is very attractive and very clever."

"Who says so?"

"I say so."

"Ho!" said Stilton. "Attractive, eh? Who does he attract?"

"Never mind whom he attracts."

"Name three people he ever attracted. And clever? He may have just about enough intelligence to open his mouth when he wants to eat, but no more. He's a halfwitted gargoyle."

"He is not a gargoyle."

"Of course he's a gargoyle. Are you going to look me in the face and deny that he wears short side-whiskers?"

"Why shouldn't he wear short side-whiskers?"

"I suppose he has to, being a louse."

"Let me tell you—"

"Oh, come on," said Stilton brusquely, and hustled her out. As they wended their way, he was reminding her once more of his Uncle Joseph's reluctance to be kept waiting for his soup.

It was a pensive Bertram Wooster, with more than a few furrows in his forehead, who returned to his chair and put match to cigarette. And I'll tell you why I was pensive and furrowed. The recent slab of dialogue between the young couple had left me extremely uneasy.

Love is a delicate plant that needs constant tending and nurturing, and this cannot be done by snorting at the adored object like a gas explosion and calling her friends lice. I had the disquieting impression that it wouldn't take too much to make the Stilton-Florence axis go p'fft again, and who could say that in this event, the latter, back in circulation, would not decide to hitch on to me once more? I remembered what had happened that other time and, as the fellow said, the burned child fears the spilled milk.

You see, the trouble with Florence was that though, as I have stated, indubitably comely and well equipped to take office as a pinup girl, she was, as I have also stressed, intellectual to the core, and the ordinary sort of bloke like myself does well to give this type of female as wide a miss as he can manage.

You know how it is with these earnest, brainy beazels of what is called strong character. They can't let the male soul alone. They want to get behind it and start shoving. Scarcely have they shaken the rice from their hair in the car driving off for the honeymoon than they pull up their socks and begin molding the partner of joys and sorrows, and if there is one thing that gives me the pip, it is being molded. Despite adverse criticism from many quarters—the name of my Aunt Agatha is one that springs to the lips—I like B. Wooster the way he is. Lay off him, I say. Don't try to change him, or you may lose the flavor.

Even when we were merely affianced, I recalled, this woman had dashed the mystery thriller from my hand, instructing me to read instead a perfectly frightful thing by a bird called Tolstoi. At the thought of what horrors might ensue after the clergyman had done his stuff and she had a legal right to bring my gray hairs in sorrow to the grave, the imagination boggled. It was a subdued and apprehensive Bertram Wooster who some moments later reached for the hat and light overcoat and went off to the Savoy to shove food into the Trotters.

The binge, as I had anticipated, did little or nothing to raise the spirits. Aunt Dahlia had not erred in stating that my guests would prove to be creeps of no common order. L. G. Trotter was a little man with a face like a weasel, who scarcely uttered during the meal because, whenever he tried to, the moon of his delight shut him up, and Mrs. Trotter was a burly heavyweight with a beaked nose who talked all the time, principally about some woman she disliked named Blenkinsop. And nothing to help me through the grim proceedings except the faint, far-off echo of those specials of Jeeves's. It was a profound relief when they finally called it a day and I was at liberty to totter off to the Drones for the restorative I so sorely needed.

The almost universal practice of the inmates being to attend some form of musical entertainment after dinner, the smoking room was empty when I arrived, and it would not be too much to say that five minutes later, a cigarette between my lips and a brimming flagon at my side, I was enveloped in a deep peace. The strained nerves had relaxed. The snootered soul was at rest.

It couldn't last, of course. These lulls in life's battle never do. Came a moment when I had that eerie feeling that I was not alone and, looking round, found myself gazing at G. D'Arcy Cheesewright.

4

THIS CHEESEWRIGHT, I should perhaps have mentioned earlier, is a bimbo who from the cradle up has devoted himself sedulously to aquatic exercise. He was Captain of Boats at Eton. He rowed four years for Oxford. He sneaks off each summer at the time of Henley Regatta and sweats lustily with his shipmates on behalf of the Leander Club. And if he ever goes to New York, I have no doubt he will squander a fortune sculling about the lake in Central Park at twenty-five cents a throw. It is only rarely that the oar is out of his hand.

Well, you can't do that sort of thing without developing the thews and sinews, and all this galley-slave stuff has left him extraordinarily robust. His chest is broad and barrel-like and the muscles of his brawny arms strong as iron bands. I remember Jeeves once speaking of someone of his acquaintance whose strength was as the strength of ten, and the description would have fitted Stilton nicely. He looks like an all-in wrestler.

Being a pretty broadminded chap and realizing that it takes all sorts to make a world, I had always till now regarded this beefiness of his with kindly toleration. The way I look at it is, if blighters want to be beefy, let them be beefy. Good luck to them, say I. What I did not like at moment of going to press was the fact that in addition to bulging in all directions with muscle he was glaring at me in a sinister manner, his air that of one of those Fiends with Hatchet who are always going about the place Slaying Six. He was plainly much stirred about something, and it would not be going too far to say that as I caught his eye, I wilted where I sat.

Thinking that it must be the circumstance of his having found me restoring the tissues with a spot of the right stuff that was causing his chagrin, I was about to say that the elixir in my hand was purely medicinal and had been recommended by a prominent Harley Street physician when he spoke.

"If only I could make up my mind!"

"About what, Stilton?"

"About whether to break your foul neck or not."

I did a bit more wilting. It seemed to me that I was alone in a deserted smoking-room with a homicidal looney. It is a type of looney I particularly bar, and the homicidal looney I like least is one with a forty-four chest and biceps in proportion. His fingers, I noticed, were twitching, always a bad sign. Oh, for the wings of a dove about summed up my feelings as I tried not to look at them.

"Break my foul neck?" I said, hoping for further information. "Why?"

"You don't know?"

"I haven't the foggiest."

"Ho!"

He paused at this point to dislodge a fly which had sauntered in through the open window and become mixed up with his vocal cords. Having achieved his object, he resumed.

"Wooster!"

"Still here, old man."

"Wooster," said Stilton, and if he wasn't grinding his teeth, I don't know a ground tooth when I see one, "what was the thought behind that moustache of yours? Why did you grow it?"

Well, rather difficult to say, of course. One gets these whims. I scratched the chin a moment.

"I suppose I felt it might brighten things up," I hazarded.

"Or had you an ulterior motive? Was it part of a subtle plot for stealing Florence from me?"

"My dear Stilton!"

"It all looks very fishy to me. Do you know what happened just now, when we left my uncle's?"

"I'm sorry, no. I'm a stranger in these parts myself."

He ground a few more teeth.

"I will tell you. I saw Florence home in a cab, and all the way there she was raving about that foul moustache of yours. It made me sick to listen to her."

I weighed the idea of saying something to the effect that girls would be girls and must be expected to have their simple enthusiasms, but decided better not.

"When we got off at her door and I turned after paying the driver, I found she was looking at me intently, examining me from every angle, her eyes fixed on my face."

"You enjoyed that, of course?"

"Shut up. Don't interrupt me."

"Right ho. I only meant it must have been pretty gratifying."

He brooded for a space. Whatever had happened at that lovers' get-together, one could see that the memory of it was stirring him like a dose of salts.

"A moment later," he said, and paused, wrestling with his feelings, "a moment later," he went on, finding speech again, "she announced that she wished me to grow a moustache, too. She said—I quote her words—that when a man has a large pink face and a head like a pumpkin, a little something around the upper lip often does wonders in the way of easing the strain. Would you say my head was like a pumpkin, Wooster?"

"Not a bit, old man."

"Not like a pumpkin?"

"No, not like a pumpkin. A touch of the dome of St. Paul's, perhaps."

"Well, that is what she compared it to, and she said that if I split it in the middle with a spot of hair, the relief to pedestrians and traffic would be enormous. She's crazy. I wore a moustache my last year at Oxford, and it looked frightful. Nearly as loathsome as yours. Moustache, forsooth!" said Stilton, which surprised me, for I hadn't supposed he knew words like "Forsooth." " 'I wouldn't grow a moustache to please a dying grandfather,' I told her. 'A nice fool I'd look with a moustache,' I said. 'It's how you look without one,' she said. 'Is that so?' I said. 'Yes, it is,' she said. 'Oh?' I said. 'Yes,' she said. 'Ho!' I said, and she said 'Ho to you!' "

If she had added "With knobs on," it would, of course, have made it stronger, but I must say I was rather impressed by Florence's work as described in this slice of dialogue. It seemed to me snappy and forceful. I suppose girls learn this sort of cut-and-thrust stuff at their finishing schools. And Florence, one must remember, had been moving a good deal of late in bohemian circles—Chelsea studios and the rooms of the intelligentsia in Bloomsbury and places like that—where the repartee is always of a high order.

"So that was that," proceeded Stilton, having brooded for a space. "One thing led to another, hot words passed to and fro, and it was not long before she was returning the ring and saying she would be glad to have her letters back at my earliest convenience."

I tut-tutted. He asked me rather abruptly not to tut-tut, so I stopped tut-tutting, explaining that my reason for having done so was that his tragic tale had moved me deeply.

"My heart aches for you," I said.

"It does, does it?"

"Profusely."

"Ho!"

"You doubt my sympathy?"

"You bet I doubt your ruddy sympathy. I told you just now that I was trying to make up my mind, and what I'm trying to make it up about is this. Had you foreseen that that would happen? Did your cunning fiend's brain spot what was bound to occur if you grew a moustache and flashed it on Florence?"

I tried to laugh lightly, but you know how it is with these light laughs, they don't always come out just the way you would wish. Even to me it sounded more like a gargle.

"Am I right? Was that the thought that came into your cunning fiend's brain?"

"Certainly not. As a matter of fact, I haven't got a cunning fiend's brain."

"Jeeves has. The plot could have been his. Was it Jeeves who wove this snare for my feet?"

"My dear chap! Jeeves doesn't weave snares for feet. He would consider it a liberty. Besides, I told you he is the spearhead of the movement which disapproves of my moustache."

"I see what you mean. Yes, on second thought I am inclined to acquit Jeeves of complicity. The evidence points to your having thought up the scheme yourself."

"Evidence? How do you mean, evidence?"

"When we were at your flat and I said I was expecting Florence, I noticed a very significant thing—your face lit up."

"It didn't."

"Pardon me. I know when a face lights up and when it doesn't. I could read you like a book. You were saying to yourself 'This is the moment! This is where I spring it on her!'"

"Nothing of the sort. If my face lit up—which I gravely doubt—it was merely because I reasoned that as soon as she arrived you would be leaving."

"You wanted me to leave?"

"I did. You were taking up space which I required for other purposes."

It was plausible, of course, and I could see it shook him. He passed a hamlike hand, gnarled with toiling at the oar, across his brow.

"Well, I shall have to think it over. Yes, yes, I shall have to think it over."

"Go away and start now, is what I would suggest."

"I will. I shall be scrupulously fair. I shall weigh this and that. But if I find my suspicions are correct, I shall know what to do about it."

And with these ominous words he withdrew, leaving me not a little bowed down with weight of woe. For apart from the fact that when a bird of Stilton's impulsive temperament gets it into his nut that you have woven snares for his feet, practically anything can happen in the way of violence and mayhem, it gave me goose pimples to think of Florence being at large once more. It was with heavy heart that I finished my whisky and splash and tottered home. "Wooster," a voice seemed to be whispering in my ear, "things are getting hot, old sport."

Jeeves was at the telephone when I reached the sitting-room.

"I am sorry," he was saying, and I noticed that he was just as suave and firm as I had been at our recent get-together. "No, please, further discussion is useless. I am afraid you must accept my decision as final. Good night."

From the fact that he had not chucked in a lot of "Sirs" I presumed that he had been talking to some pal of his, though from the curtness of his tone probably not the one whose strength was as the strength of ten.

"What was that, Jeeves?" I asked. "A little tiff with one of the boys at the club?"

"No, sir. I was speaking to Mr. Percy Gorringe, who rang up shortly before you entered. Affecting to be yourself, I informed him that his request for a thousand pounds could not be entertained. I thought that this might spare you discomfort and embarrassment."

I must say I was touched. After being worsted in that clash of wills of ours, one might have expected him to show dudgeon and be loath to do the feudal thing by the young master. But Jeeves and I, though we may have our differences—as it might be on the subject of lip-joy—do not allow them to rankle.

"Thank you, Jeeves."

"Not at all, sir."

"Lucky you came back in time to do the needful. Did you enjoy yourself at the club?"

"Very much, sir."

"More than I did at mine."

"Sir?"

"I ran into Stilton Cheesewright there and found him in difficult mood. Tell me, Jeeves, what do you do at this Junior Ganymede of yours?"

"Well, sir, many of the members play a sound game of bridge. The conversation, too, is always of a high order. And should one desire more frivolous entertainment, there is the club book."

"The . . . oh, yes, I remember."

Perhaps you do, too, if you happened to be around when I was relating the doings at Totleigh Towers, the country seat of Sir Watkyn Bassett, when this club book had enabled me to put it so crushingly across the powers of darkness in the shape of Roderick Spode. Under Rule Eleven at the Junior Ganymede, you may recall, members are required to supply intimate details concerning their employers for inclusion in the volume, and its pages revealed that Spode, who was an amateur Dictator of sorts, running a gang called the Black Shorts, who went about in black footer bags shouting "Heil, Spode!," also secretly designed ladies' underclothing under the trade name of Eulalie Soeurs. Armed with this knowledge, I had had, of course, little difficulty in reducing him to the level of a third-class power. These Dictators don't want a thing like that to get spread about.

But though the club book had served me well on that occasion, I was far from approving of it. Mine has been in many ways a checkered career, and it was not pleasant to think that full details of episodes I would prefer to be buried in oblivion were giving a big laugh daily to a bunch of valets and butlers.

"You couldn't tear the Wooster material out of that club book, could you, Jeeves?"

"I fear not, sir."

"It contains matter that can fairly be described as dynamite."

"Very true, sir."

"Suppose the contents were bruited about and reached the ears of my Aunt Agatha?"

"You need have no concern on that point, sir. Each member fully understands that perfect discretion is a *sine qua non*."

"All the same I'd feel happier if that page—"

"Those eleven pages, sir."

"—if those eleven pages were consigned to the flames." A sudden thought struck me. "Is there anything about Stilton Cheesewright in the book?"

"A certain amount, sir."

"Damaging?"

"Not in any real sense of the word, sir. His personal attendant merely reports that he has a habit, when moved, of saying 'Ho!' and does Swedish exercises in the nude each morning before breakfast."

I sighed. I hadn't really hoped, and yet it had been a disappointment. I have always held—rightly, I think—that nothing eases the tension of a difficult situation like a well-spotted bit of blackmail, and it would have been agreeable to have been in a position to go to Stilton and say "Cheesewright, I know your secret!" and watch him wilt. But you can't fulfill yourself to any real extent in that direction if all the party of the second part does is say "Ho!" and tie himself into knots before sailing into the eggs and b. It was plain that with Stilton there could be no such moral triumph as I had achieved in the case of Roderick Spode.

"Ah, well," I said resignedly, "if that's that, that's that, what?"

"So it would appear, sir."

"Nothing to do but keep the chin up and the upper lip as stiff as can be managed. I think I'll go to bed with an improving book. Have you read *The Mystery of the Pink Crayfish* by Rex West?"

"No, sir, I have not enjoyed that experience. Oh, pardon me, sir, I was forgetting. Lady Florence Craye spoke to me on the telephone shortly before you came in. Her ladyship would be glad if you would ring her up. I will get the number, sir."

I was puzzled. I could make nothing of this. No reason, of course, why she shouldn't want me to give her a buzz, but on the other hand no reason that I could see why she should.

"She didn't say what she wanted?"

"No, sir."

"Odd, Jeeves."

"Yes, sir. . . . One moment, m'lady. Here is Mr. Wooster."

I took the instrument from him and hullo-ed.

"Bertie?"

"On the spot."

"I hope you weren't in bed?"

"No, no."

"I thought you wouldn't be. Bertie, will you do something for me? I want you to take me to a night club tonight."

"Eh?"

"A night club. Rather a low one. I mean garish and all that sort of thing. It's for the book I'm writing. Atmosphere."

"Oh, ah," I said, enlightened. I knew all about this atmosphere thing. Bingo Little's wife, the well-known novelist Rosie M. Banks, is as hot as a pistol on it, Bingo has often told me. She frequently sends him off to take notes of this and that so that she shall have plenty of ammo for her next chapter. If you're a novelist, apparently, you have to get your atmosphere correct, or your public starts writing you stinkers beginning "Dear Madam, are you aware . . . ?" "You're doing something about a night club?"

"Yes, I'm just coming to the part where my hero goes to one, and I've never been to any except the respectable ones where everybody goes, which aren't the sort of thing I want. What I need is something more—"

"Garish?"

"Yes, garish."

"You want to go tonight?"

"It must be tonight, because I'm off tomorrow afternoon to Brinkley."

"Oh, you're going to stay with Aunt Dahlia?"

"Yes. Well, can you manage it?"

"Oh, rather. Delighted."

"Good. D'Arcy Cheesewright," said Florence, and I noted the steely what-d'you-call-it in her voice, "was to have taken me, but he finds himself unable to. So I've had to fall back on you."

This might, I thought, have been more tactfully put, but I let it go.

"Right ho," I said. "I'll call for you at about half-past eleven."

You are surprised? You are saying to yourself "Come, come, Wooster, what's all this?" wondering why I was letting myself in for a beano from which I might well have shrunk? The matter is susceptible of a ready explanation.

My quick mind, you see, had spotted instantly that this was where I might quite conceivably do myself a bit of good. Having mellowed this girl with food and drink, who knew but that I might succeed in effecting a reconciliation between her and the piece of cheese with whom until tonight she had been headed for the altar rails, thus averting the peril which must always loom on the Wooster horizon while she remained unattached and at a loose end? It needed, I was convinced, only a few kindly words from a sympathetic man of the world, and these I was prepared to supply in full measure.

"Jeeves," I said, "I shall be going out again. This will mean having to postpone finishing the mystery of the pink crayfish to a later date, but that can't be helped. As a matter of fact, I rather fancy I have already wrested its secret from it. Unless I am very much mistaken, the man who bumped off Sir Eustace Willoughby, Bart., was the butler."

"Indeed, sir?"

"That is what I think, having sifted the clues. All that stuff throwing suspicion on the vicar doesn't fool me for an instant. Will you ring up The Mottled Oyster and book a table in my name."

"Not too near the band, sir?"

"How right you are, Jeeves. Not too near the band."

5

I DON'T KNOW why it is, but I'm not much of a lad for night clubs these days. Age creeping on me, I suppose. But I still retain my membership in about half a dozen, including this Mottled Oyster at which I had directed Jeeves to book me a table.

The old spot has passed a somewhat restless existence since I first joined, and from time to time I get a civil note from its proprietors saying that it has changed its name and address once more. When it was raided as The Feverish Cheese, it became The Frozen Limit, and when it was raided as The Frozen Limit, it bore for a while mid snow and ice the banner with the strange device The Startled Shrimp. From that to The Mottled Oyster was, of course, but a step. In my hot youth I had passed not a few quite pleasant evenings beneath its roof in its various incarnations, and I thought that if it preserved anything approaching the old form, it ought to be garish enough to suit Florence. As I remembered, it rather prided itself on its garishness. That was why the rozzers were always raiding it.

I picked her up at her flat at eleven-thirty, and found her in somber mood, the lips compressed, the eyes inclined to gaze into space with a sort of hard glow in them. No doubt something along these lines is always the aftermath of a brisk dust-up with the heart-throb. During the taxi drive she remained *sotto voce* and the silent tomb, and from the way her foot kept tapping on the floor of the vehicle I knew that she was thinking of Stilton, whether or not in agony of spirit I was, of course, unable to say, but I thought it probable. Following her into the joint, I was on the whole optimistic. It seemed to me that with any luck I ought to be successful in the task that lay before me—viz. softening her with well-chosen words and jerking her better self back to the surface.

When we took our seats and I looked about me, I must confess that, having this object in mind, I could have done with dimmer lights and a more romantic *tout ensemble,* if *tout ensemble* is the expression I want. I could also have dispensed with the rather strong smell of kippered herrings which hung over the establishment like a fog. But against these drawbacks could be set the fact that up on the platform where the band was, a man with adenoids was singing through a megaphone and, like all men who sing through megaphones nowadays, ladling out stuff well calculated to melt the hardest heart.

It's an odd thing. I know one or two song writers and have found them among the most cheery of my acquaintances, ready of smile and full of merry quips and so forth. But directly they put pen to paper they never fail to take the dark view. All that We're-drifting-apart-you're-breaking-my-heart stuff, I mean to say. The thing this bird was putting across per megaphone at the moment was about a chap crying into his pillow because the girl he loved was getting married next day, but—and this was the point or nub—not to him. He didn't like it. He viewed the situation with concern. And the megaphonist was extracting every ounce of juice from the setup.

Some fellows, no doubt, would have taken advantage of this outstanding goo to plunge without delay into what Jeeves calls *medias res,* but I, being shrewd, knew that you have to give these things time to work. So, having ordered kippers and a bottle of what would probably turn out to be rat poison, I opened the conversation on a more restrained note, asking her how the new novel was coming along. Authors, especially when female, like to keep you posted about this.

She said it was coming along very well but not quickly, because she was a slow, careful worker who mused a good bit in between paragraphs and spared no pains to find the exact word with which to express what she wished to say. Like Flaubert, she said, and I said I thought she was on the right lines.

"Those," I said, "were more or less my methods when I wrote that thing of mine for the *Boudoir.*"

I was alluding to the weekly paper for the delicately nurtured, *Milady's Boudoir,* of which Aunt Dahlia is the courteous and popular proprietor or proprietress. She has been running it now for about three years, a good deal to the annoyance of Uncle Tom, her husband, who has to foot the bills. At her request I had once contributed an article—or "piece," as we journalists call it—on What the Well-Dressed Man Is Wearing.

"So you're off to Brinkley tomorrow," I went on. "You'll like that. Fresh air, gravel soil, company's own water, Anatole's cooking and so forth."

"Yes. And of course it will be wonderful meeting Daphne Dolores Morehead."

The name was new to me.

"Daphne Dolores Morehead?"

"The novelist. She is going to be there. I admire her work so much. I see, by the way, she is doing a serial for the *Boudoir*."

"Oh, yes?" I said, intrigued. One always likes to hear about the activities of one's fellow-writers.

"It must have cost your aunt a fortune. Daphne Dolores Morehead is frightfully expensive. I can't remember what it is she gets a thousand words, but it's something enormous."

"The old sheet must be doing well."

"I suppose so."

She spoke listlessly, seeming to have lost interest in *Milady's Boudoir*. Her thoughts, no doubt, had returned to Stilton. She cast a dull eye hither and thither about the room. It had begun to fill up now, and the dance floor was congested with frightful bounders of both sexes.

"What horrible people," she said. "I must say I am surprised that you should be familiar with such places, Bertie. Are they all like this?"

I weighed the question.

"Well, some are better and some worse. I would call this one about average. Garish, of course, but then you said you wanted something garish."

"Oh, I'm not complaining. I shall make some useful notes. It is just the sort of place to which I pictured Rollo going that night."

"Rollo?"

"The hero of my novel. Rollo Beaminster."

"Oh, I see. Yes, of course. Out on the tiles, was he?"

"He was in wild mood. Reckless. Desperate. He had lost the girl he loved."

"What ho!" I said. "Tell me more."

I spoke with animation and vim, for whatever you may say of Bertram Wooster, you cannot say that he does not know a cue when he hears one. Throw him the line, and he will do the rest. I hitched up the larynx. The kippers and the bot had arrived by now, and I took a mouthful of the former and a sip of the latter. It tasted like hair-oil.

"You interest me strangely," I said. "Lost the girl he loved, had he?"

"She had told him she never wished to see or speak to him again."

"Well, well. Always a nasty knock for a chap, that."

"So he comes to this low night club. He is trying to forget."

"But I'll bet he doesn't."

"No, it is useless. He looks about him at the glitter and garishness and feels how hollow it all is. I think I can use that waiter over there in the night club scene, the one with the watery eyes and the pimple on his nose," she said, jotting down a note on the back of the bill of fare. She was plainly collecting some useful material.

I fortified myself with a swig of whatever the stuff was in the bottle and prepared to give her the works.

"Always a mistake," I said, starting to do the sympathetic man of the world, "fellows losing girls and—conversely— girls losing fellows. I don't know how you feel about it, but the way it seems to me is that it's a silly idea giving the dream man the raspberry just because of some trifling tiff. Kiss and make up, I always say. I saw Stilton at the Drones tonight," I said, getting down to it.

She stiffened and took a reserved mouthful of kipper. Her voice, when the consignment had passed down the hatch and she was able to speak, was cold and metallic.

"Oh, yes?"

"He was in wild mood."

"Oh, yes?"

"Reckless. Desperate. He looked about him at the Drones smoking-room, and I could see he was feeling what a hollow smoking-room it was."

"Oh, yes?"

Well, I suppose if someone had come along at this moment and said to me "Hullo there, Wooster, how's it going? Are you making headway?" I should have had to reply in the negative. "Not perceptibly, Wilkinson,"—or Banks or Smith or Knatchbull-Huguessen or whatever the name might have been, I would have said. I had the uncomfortable feeling of having been laid a stymie. However, I persevered.

"Yes, he was in quite a state of mind. He gave me the impression that it wouldn't take much to make him go off to the Rocky Mountains and shoot grizzly bears. Not a pleasant thought."

"You mean if one is fond of grizzly bears?"

"I was thinking more if one was fond of Stiltons."

"I'm not."

"Oh? Well, suppose he joined the Foreign Legion?"

"It would have my sympathy."

"You wouldn't like to think of him tramping through the hot sand without a pub in sight, with Riffs or whatever they're called potting at him from all directions."

"Yes, I would. If I saw a Riff trying to shoot D'Arcy Cheesewright, I would hold his hat for him and egg him on."

Once more I had that sense of not making progress. Her face, I observed, was cold and hard, like my kipper, which of course during these exchanges I had been neglecting, and I began to understand how those birds in Holy Writ must have felt after their session with the deaf adder. I can't recall all the details, though at my private school I once won a prize for Scripture Knowledge, but I remember that they had the dickens of an uphill job trying to charm it, and after they had sweated themselves to a frazzle no business resulted. It is often this way, I believe, with deaf adders.

"Do you know Horace Pendlebury-Davenport?" I said, after a longish pause during which we worked away at our respective kippers.

"The man who married Valerie Twistleton?"

"That's the chap. Formerly the Drones Club Darts champion."

"I've met him. But why bring him up?"

"Because he points the moral and adorns the tale. During the period of their betrothal he and Valerie had a row similar in caliber to that which has occurred between you and Stilton and pretty nearly parted forever."

She gave me the frosty eye.

"Must we talk about Mr. Cheesewright?"

"I see him as tonight's big topic."

"I don't, and I think I'll go home."

"Oh, not yet. I want to tell you about Horace and Valerie. They had this row of which I speak and might, as I say, have parted forever, had they not been reconciled by a woman who, so Horace says, looked as if she bred cocker spaniels. She told them a touching story, which melted their hearts. She said she had once loved a bloke and quarreled with him about some trifle, and he turned on his heel and went off to the Federated Malay States and married the widow of a rubber planter. And each year from then on there arrived at her address a simple posy of white violets, together with a slip of paper bearing the words 'It might have been.' You wouldn't like that to happen with you and Stilton, would you?"

"I'd love it."

"It doesn't give you a pang to think that at this very moment he may be going the rounds of the shipping offices, inquiring about sailings to the Malay States?"

"They'd be shut at this time of night."

"Well, first thing tomorrow morning, then."

She laid down her knife and fork and gave me an odd look.

"Bertie, you're extraordinary," she said.

"Eh? How do you mean, extraordinary?"

"All this nonsense you have been talking, trying to reconcile me and D'Arcy. Not that I don't admire you for it. I think it's rather wonderful of you. But then everybody says that though you have a brain like a peahen, you're the soul of kindness and generosity."

Well, I was handicapped here by the fact that, never having met a peahen, I was unable to estimate the quality of these fowls' intelligence, but she had spoken as if they were a bit short of the gray matter, and I was about to ask her who the hell she meant by "everybody," when she resumed.

"You want to marry me yourself, don't you?"

I had to take another mouthful of the hell-brew before I could speak. One of those difficult questions to answer.

"Oh, rather," I said, for I was anxious to make the evening a success. "Of course. Who wouldn't?"

"And yet you—"

She did not proceed further than the word "you," for at this juncture, with the abruptness with which these things always happen, the joint was pinched. The band stopped in the middle of a bar. A sudden hush fell upon the room.

Square-jawed men shot up through the flooring, and one, who seemed to be skippering the team, stood out in the middle and in a voice like a foghorn told everybody to keep their seats. I remember thinking how nicely timed the whole thing was—breaking loose, I mean, at a moment when the conversation had taken a distasteful turn and threatened to become fraught with embarrassment. I have heard hard things said about the London police force— notably by Catsmeat Potter-Pirbright and others on the morning after the annual Oxford and Cambridge boat race—but a fairminded man had to admit that there were occasions when they showed tact of no slight order.

I wasn't alarmed, of course. I had been through this sort of thing many a time and oft, as the expression is, and I knew what happened. So, noting that my guest was giving a rather close imitation of a cat on hot bricks, I hastened to dispel her alarm.

"No need to get the breeze up," I said. "Nothing is here for tears, nothing to wail or knock the breast," I added, using one of Jeeves's gags which I chanced to remember. "Everything is quite in order."

"But won't they arrest us?"

I laughed lightly. These novices!

"Absurd. No danger of that whatsoever."

"How do you know?"

"All this is old stuff to me. Here in a nutshell is the pro- cedure. They round us up, and we push off in an orderly manner to the police station in plain vans. There we assemble in the waiting-room and give our names and addresses, exercising a certain latitude as regards the details. I, for example, generally call myself Ephraim Gadsby of The Nasturtiums, Jubilee Road, Streatham Common. I don't know why. Just a whim. You, if you will be guided by me, will be Matilda Bott of 365 Churchill Avenue, East Dulwich. These formalities concluded, we shall be free to depart, leaving the proprietor to face the awful majesty of Justice."

She refused to be consoled. The resemblance to a cat on hot bricks became more marked. Though instructed by the foghorn chap to keep her seat, she shot up as if a spike had come through it.

"I'm sure that's not what happens."

"It is, unless they've changed the rules."

"You have to appear in court."

"No, no."

"Well, I'm not going to risk it. Good night."

And getting smoothly off the mark she made a dash for the service door, which was not far from where we sat. And an adjacent constable, baying like a bloodhound, started off in hot pursuit.

Whether I acted judiciously at this point is a question which I have never been able to decide. Sometimes I think yes, reflecting that the Chevalier Bayard in my place would have done the same, sometimes no. Briefly what occurred was that as the gendarme came galloping by, I shoved out a foot, causing him to take the toss of a lifetime. Florence withdrew, and the guardian of the peace, having removed his left boot from his right ear, with which it had become temporarily entangled, rose and informed me that I was in custody.

As at the moment he was grasping the scruff of my neck with one hand and the seat of my trousers with the other, I saw no reason to doubt the honest fellow.

6

I SPENT THE NIGHT in what is called durance vile, and bright and early next day was haled before the beak at Vinton Street police court, charged with assaulting an officer of the law and impeding him in the execution of his duties, which I suppose was a fairly neat way of putting it. I was extremely hungry and needed a shave.

It was the first time I had met the Vinton Street chap, always hitherto having patronized his trade rival at Bosher Street, but Barmy Fotheringay-Phipps, who was introduced to him on the morning of January the first one year, had told me he was a man to avoid, and the truth of this was now borne in upon me in no uncertain manner. It seemed to me, as I stood listening to the cop running through the story sequence, that Barmy, in describing this Solon as a twenty-minute egg with many of the less lovable qualities of some high-up official of the Spanish Inquisition, had understated rather than exaggerated the facts.

I didn't like the look of the old blister at all. His manner was austere, and as the tale proceeded his face, such as it was, grew hard and dark with menace. He kept shooting quick glances at me through his pince-nez, and the dullest eye could see that the constable was getting all the sympathy of the audience and that the citizen cast for the role of Heavy in this treatment was the prisoner Gadsby. More and more the feeling stole over me that the prisoner Gadsby was about to get it in the gizzard and would be lucky if he didn't fetch up on Devil's Island.

However, when the *J'accuse* stuff was over and I was asked if I had anything to say, I did my best. I admitted that on the occasion about which we had been chatting I had extended a foot, causing the officer to go base over apex, but protested that it had been a pure accident without any *arrière pensée* on my part. I said I had been feeling cramped after a longish sojourn at the table and had merely desired to unlimber the leg muscles.

"You know how sometimes you want a stretch," I said.

"I am strongly inclined," responded the beak, "to give you one. A good long stretch."

Rightly recognizing this as comedy, I uttered a cordial guffaw to show that my heart was in the right place, and an officious blighter in the well of the court shouted "Silence!" I tried to explain that I was convulsed by His Worship's ready wit, but he shushed me again, and His Worship came to the surface once more.

"However," he went on, adjusting his pince-nez, "in consideration of your youth I will exercise clemency."

"Oh, fine," I said.

"Fine," replied the other half of the cross-talk act, who seemed to know all the answers, "is right. Ten pounds. Next case."

I paid my debt to Society, and pushed off.

Jeeves was earning the weekly envelope by busying himself at some domestic task when I reached the old home. He cocked an inquiring eye at me, and I felt that an explanation was due him. It would have surprised him, of course, to discover that my room was empty and my bed had not been slept in.

"A little trouble last night with the minions of the law, Jeeves," I said. "Quite a bit of that Eugene-Aram-Walked-between-with-gyves-upon-his-wrists stuff."

"Indeed, sir? Most vexing."

"Yes, I didn't like it much, but the magistrate—with whom I have just been threshing the thing out—had a wonderful time. I brought a ray of sunshine into his drab life, all right. Did you know that these magistrates were expert comedians?"

"No, sir. The fact had not been drawn to my attention."

"Think of Groucho Marx and you will get the idea. One gag after another, and all at my expense. I was just the straight man, and I found the experience most unpleasant, particularly as I had had no breakfast that any conscientious gourmet could call breakfast. Have you ever passed the night in chokey, Jeeves?"

"No, sir. I have been fortunate in that respect."

"It renders the appetite unusually keen. So rally round, if you don't mind, and busy yourself with the skillet. We have eggs on the premises, I presume?"

"Yes, sir."

"I shall need about fifty, fried, with perhaps the same number of pounds of bacon. Toast, also. Four loaves will probably be sufficient, but stand by to weigh in with more if necessary. And don't forget the coffee—say sixteen pots."

"Very good, sir."

"And after that," I said with a touch of bitterness, "I suppose you will go racing round to the Junior Ganymede to enter this spot of bother of mine in the club book."

"I fear I have no alternative, sir. Rule Eleven is very strict."

"Well, if you must, you must, I suppose. I wouldn't want you to be hauled up in a hollow square of butlers and have your buttons snipped off. That club book, Jeeves. You're absolutely sure there's nothing in it in the C's under 'Cheesewright'?"

"Nothing but what I outlined last night, sir."

"And a lot of help that is," I said moodily. "I don't mind telling you, Jeeves, that this Cheesewright has become a menace."

"Indeed, sir?"

"And I had hoped that you might have found something in the club book which would have enabled me to spike his guns. Still, if you can't, you can't, of course. All right, rush along and dish up that breakfast."

I had slept but fitfully on the plank bed which was all that the Vinton Street Gestapo had seen their way to provide for the use of clients, so after partaking of a hearty meal I turned in between the sheets. Like Rollo Beaminster, I wanted to forget. It must have been well after the luncheon hour when the sound of the telephone jerked me out of the dreamless. Feeling a good deal refreshed, I shoved on a dressing gown and went to the instrument.

It was Florence.

"Bertie?" she yipped.

"Hullo? I thought you said you were going to Brinkley today."

"I'm just starting. I rang up to ask how you got on after I left last night."

I laughed a mirthless laugh.

"Not so frightfully well," I replied. "I was scooped in by the constabulary."

"What! You told me they didn't arrest you."

"They don't. But they did."

"Are you all right now?"

"Well, I have a pinched look."

"But I don't understand. Why did they arrest you?"

"It's a long story. Cutting it down to the gist, I noticed that you were anxious to leave, so, observing that a rozzer was after you hell-for-leather, I put a foot out, tripping him up and causing him to lose interest in the chase."

"Good gracious!"

"It seemed to me the prudent policy to pursue. Another moment and he would have had you by the seat of the pants, and of course we can't have that sort of thing going on. The upshot of the affair was that I spent the night in a prison cell and had rather a testing morning with the magistrate at Vinton Street police court. However, I'm pulling round all right."

"Oh, Bertie!" Seeming deeply moved, she thanked me brokenly, and I said Don't mention it. Then she gasped a sudden gasp, as if she had received a punch on the third waistcoat button. "Did you say Vinton Street?"

"That's right."

"Oh, my goodness. Do you know who that magistrate was?"

"I couldn't tell you. No cards were exchanged. We boys in court called him Your Worship."

"He's D'Arcy's uncle!"

I goshed. It had startled me not a little.

"You don't mean that?"

"Yes."

"What, the one who likes soup?"

"Yes. Just imagine if after having dinner with him last night I had appeared before him in the dock this morning!"

"Embarrassing. Difficult to know what to say."

"D'Arcy would never have forgiven me."

"Eh?"

"He would have broken the engagement."

I didn't get this.

"How do you mean?"

"How do I mean what?"

"How do you mean he would have broken the engagement? I thought it was off already."

She gave what I believe is usually called a rippling laugh.

"Oh, no. He rang me up this morning and climbed down. And I forgave him. He's starting to grow a moustache today."

I was profoundly relieved.

"Well, that's splendid," I said, and when she Oh-Bertie-ed and I asked her what she was Oh-Bertie-ing about, she explained that what she had had in mind was the fact that I was so chivalrous and generous.

"Not many men in your place, feeling as you do about me, would behave like this."

"Quite all right."

"I'm very touched."

"Don't give it another thought. It's really all on again, is it?"

"Yes. So mind you don't breathe a word to him about my being at that place with you."

"Of course not."

"D'Arcy is so jealous."

"Exactly. He must never know."

"Never. Why, if he even found out I was telephoning to you now, he would have a fit."

I was about to laugh indulgently and say that this was

what Jeeves calls a remote contingency, because how the dickens could he ever learn that we had been chewing the fat, when my eye was attracted by a large object just within my range of vision. Slewing the old bean round a couple of inches, I was enabled to perceive that this large o. was the bulging form of G. D'Arcy Cheesewright. I hadn't heard the door bell ring, and I hadn't seen him come in, but there unquestionably he was, haunting the place once more like a resident specter.

7

IT WAS A MOMENT for quick thinking. One doesn't want fellows having fits all over one's sitting-room. I was extremely dubious, moreover, as to whether, should he ascertain who was at the other end of the wire, he would confine himself to fits.

"Certainly, Catsmeat," I said. "Of course, Catsmeat. I quite understand, Catsmeat. But I'll have to ring off now, Catsmeat, as our mutual friend Cheesewright has just come in. Goodbye, Catsmeat." I hung up the receiver and turned to Stilton. "That was Catsmeat," I said.

He made no comment on this information, but stood glowering darkly. Now that I had been apprised of the ties of blood linking him with mine host of Vinton Street, I could see the family resemblance. Both uncle and nephew had the same way of narrowing their gaze and letting you have it from beneath the overhanging eyebrow. The only difference was that whereas the former pierced you to the roots of the soul through rimless pince-nez, with the latter you got the eye nude.

For a moment I was under the impression that my visitor's emotion was due to his having found me at this advanced hour in pyjamas and a dressing gown, a costume which, if worn at three o'clock in the afternoon, is always liable to start a train of thought. But it seemed that this was not so. More serious matters were on the agenda paper.

"Wooster," he said, in a rumbling voice like the Cornish express going through a tunnel, "where were you last night?"

I own the question rattled me. For an instant, indeed, I rocked on my base. Then I reminded myself that nothing could be proved against me, and was strong again.

"Ah, Stilton," I said cheerily, "come in, come in. Oh, you are in, aren't you? Well, take a seat and tell me all your news. A lovely day, is it not? You'll find a lot of people who don't like July in London, but I am all for it myself. It always seems to me there's a certain sort of something about it."

He appeared to be one of those fellows who are not interested in July in London, for he showed no disposition to pursue the subject, merely giving one of those snorts of his.

"Where were you last night, you blighted louse?" he said, and I noticed that the face was suffused, the cheek muscles twitching and the eyes, like stars, starting from their spheres.

I had a pop at being cool and nonchalant.

"Last night?" I said, musing. "Let me see, that would be the night of July the twenty-second, would it not? H'm. Ha. The night of—"

He swallowed a couple of times.

"I see you have forgotten. Let me assist your memory. You were in a low night club with Florence Craye, my fiancée."

"Who, me?"

"Yes, you. And this morning you were in the dock at Vinton Street police court."

"You're sure you mean me?"

"Quite sure. I had the information from my uncle, who is the magistrate there. He came to lunch at my flat today, and as he was leaving he caught sight of your photograph on the wall."

"I didn't know you kept my photograph on your wall, Stilton. I'm touched."

He continued to ferment.

"It was a group photograph," he said curtly, "and you happened to be in it. He looked at it, sniffed sharply and said 'Do you know this young man?' I explained that we belonged to the same club, so it was not always possible to avoid you, but that that was the extent of our association. I was going on to say that, left to myself, I wouldn't touch you with a ten-foot pole, when he proceeded. Still sniffing, he said he was glad I was not a close friend of yours, because you weren't at all the sort of fellow he liked to think of any nephew of his being matey with. He said you had been up before him this morning, charged with assaulting a policeman, who stated that he had arrested you for tripping him up while he was chasing a girl with platinum hair in a night club."

I pursed the lips. Or, rather I tried to, but something seemed to have gone wrong with the machinery. Still, I spoke boldly and with spirit.

"Indeed?" I said. "Personally I would be inclined to attach little credence to the word of the sort of policeman who spends his time chasing platinum-haired girls in night clubs. And as for this uncle of yours, with his wild stories of me having been up before him—well, you know what magistrates are. The lowest form of pond life. When a fellow hasn't the brains and initiative to sell jellied eels, they make him a magistrate."

"You mean that when he said that about your photograph he was deceived by some slight resemblance?"

I waved a hand.

"Not necessarily a slight resemblance. London's full of chaps who look like me. I'm a very common type. People have told me that there is a fellow called Ephraim Gadsby—one of the Streatham Common Gadsbys—who is positively my double. I shall, of course, take this into consideration when weighing the question of bringing an action for slander and defamation of character against this uncle of yours, and shall probably decide to let justice be tempered with mercy. But it would be a kindly act to warn the old son of a bachelor to be more careful in future how he allows his tongue to run away with him. There are limits to one's forbearance."

He brooded darkly for about forty-five seconds.

"Platinum hair, the policeman said," he observed at the end of this lull. "This girl had platinum hair."

"No doubt very becoming."

"I find it extremely significant that Florence has platinum hair."

"I don't see why. Hundreds of girls have. My dear Stilton, ask yourself if it is likely that Florence would have been at a night club like the . . . what did you say the name was?"

"I didn't. But I believe it was called The Mottled Oyster."

"Ah, yes, I have heard of it. Not a very nice place, I understand. Quite incredible that she would have gone to a joint like that. A fastidious, intellectual girl like Florence? No, no."

He pondered. It seemed to me that I had him going.

"She wanted me to take her to a night club last night," he said. "Something to do with getting material for her new book."

"But you very properly refused?"

"No, as a matter of fact, I said I would. Then we had that bit of trouble, so of course it was off."

"And she, of course, went home to bed. What else would any pure, sweet English girl have done? It amazes me that you can suppose even for a moment that she would have gone to one of these dubious establishments without you. Especially a place where, as I understand your story, squads of policemen are incessantly chasing platinum-haired girls hither and thither, and probably even worse things happening as the long night wears on. No, Stilton, dismiss these thoughts—which, if you will allow me to say so, are unworthy of you—and . . . Ah, here is Jeeves," I said, noting with relief that the sterling fellow, who had just oozed in, was carrying the old familiar shaker. "What have you there, Jeeves? Some of your specials?"

"Yes, sir. I fancied that Mr. Cheesewright might possibly be glad of refreshment."

"He's just in the vein for it. I won't join you, Stilton, because, as you know, with this Darts tournament coming on, I am in more or less strict training these days, but I must insist on your trying one of these superb mixtures of Jeeves's. You have been anxious . . . worried . . . disturbed . . . and it will pull you together. Oh, by the way, Jeeves."

"Sir?"

"I wonder if you remember, when I came home last night after chatting with Mr. Cheesewright at the Drones, my saying to you that I was going straight to bed with an improving book?"

"Certainly, sir."

"*The Mystery of the Pink Crayfish,* was it not?"

"Precisely, sir."

"I think I said something to the effect that I could hardly wait till I could get at it?"

"As I recollect, those were your exact words, sir. You were, you said, counting the minutes until you could curl up with it."

"Thank you, Jeeves."

"Not at all, sir."

He oozed off, and I turned to Stilton, throwing the arms out in a sort of wide gesture. I don't suppose I have ever come closer in my life to saying "*Voilà!*"

"You heard?" I said. "If that doesn't leave me without a stain on my character, it is difficult to see what it does leave me without. But let me help you to your special. You will find it rare and refreshing."

It's a curious thing about those specials of Jeeves's, and one on which many revelers have commented, that while, as I mentioned earlier, they wake the sleeping tiger in you, they also work the other way round. I mean, if the tiger in you isn't sleeping but on the contrary up and doing with a heart for any fate, they lull it. You come in like a lion, you take your snootful, and you got out like a lamb. Impossible to explain it, of course. One can merely state the facts.

It was so now with Stilton. In his pre-special phase he had been all steamed up and fit for treasons, stratagems and spoils, as the fellow said, and he became a better, kindlier man beneath my very gaze. Halfway through the initial snifter he was admitting in the friendliest way that he had wronged me. I might be the most consummate ass that ever eluded the vigilance of the talent scouts of Colney Hatch, he said, but it was obvious that I had not taken

Florence to The Mottled Oyster. And dashed lucky for me I hadn't, he added, for had such been the case, he would have broken my spine in three places. In short, all very chummy and cordial.

"Harking back to the earlier portion of our conversation, Stilton," I said, changing the subject after we had agreed that his Uncle Joseph was a cockeyed fathead who would do well to consult some good oculist, "I noticed that when you spoke of Florence, you used the expression 'My fiancée.' Am I to infer from this that the dove of peace has pulled a quick one since I saw you last? That broken engagement, has it been soldered?"

He nodded.

"Yes," he said. "I made certain concessions and yielded certain points." Here his hand strayed to his upper lip and a look of pain passed over his face. "A reconciliation took place this morning."

"Splendid!"

"You're pleased?"

"Of course."

"Ho!"

"Eh?"

He eyed me fixedly.

"Wooster, come off it. You know you're in love with her yourself."

"Absurd."

"Absurd, my foot. You needn't think you can fool me. You worship that girl, and I am still inclined to believe that the whole of this moustache sequence was a vile plot on your part to steal her from me. Well, all I have to say is that if I ever catch you oiling round her and trying to alienate her affections, I shall break your spine in four places."

"Three, I thought you said."

71

"No, four. However, she will be out of your reach for some little time, I am glad to say. She goes today to visit your aunt, Mrs. Travers, in Worcestershire."

Amazing how with a careless word you can land yourself in the soup. I was within the merest toucher of saying Yes, so she had told me, which would, of course, have been fatal. In the nick of time I contrived to substitute an "Oh, really?"

"She's going to Brinkley, is she? You also?"

"I shall be following in a few days."

"You aren't going with her?"

"Talk sense. You don't suppose I intend to appear in public during the early stages of growing that damned moustache she insists on. I shall remain confined to my room till the foul thing has started to sprout a bit. Goodbye, Wooster. You will remember what I was saying about your spine?"

I assured him that I would bear it in mind, and he finished his special and withdrew.

8

THE DAYS THAT FOLLOWED saw me at the peak of my form, fizzy to an almost unbelievable extent and enchanting one and all with my bright smile and merry sallies. During this halcyon period, if halcyon is the word I want, it would not be too much to say that I revived like a watered flower.

It was as if a great weight had been rolled off the soul. Only those who have had to endure the ordeal of having G. D'Arcy Cheesewright constantly materialize from thin air and steal up behind them, breathing down the back of their necks as they took their ease in their smoking-room, can fully understand the relief of being able to sink into a chair and order a restorative, knowing that the place would be wholly free from this pre-eminent scourge. My feelings, I suppose, were roughly what those of Mary would have been, had she looked over her shoulder one morning and found the lamb no longer among those present.

And then—*bing*—just as I was saying to myself that this was the life, along came all those telegrams.

The first to arrive reached me at my residence just as I was lighting the after-breakfast cigarette, and I eyed it with something of the nervous discomfort of one confronted with a ticking bomb. Telegrams have so often been

the heralds or harbingers or whatever they're called of
sharp crises in my affairs that I have come to look on them
askance, wondering if something is going to pop out of the
envelope and bite me in the leg. It was with a telegram, it
may be recalled, that Fate teed off in the sinister episode of
Sir Watkyn Bassett, Roderick Spode and the silver cow-
creamer which I was instructed by Aunt Dahlia to pinch
from the first-named's collection at Totleigh Towers.

Little wonder, then, that as I brooded over this one—
eyeing it, as I say, askance—I was asking myself if Hell's
foundations were about to quiver again.

Still, there the thing was, and it seemed to me, weighing the pros and cons, that only one course lay before
me—viz. to open it.

I did so. Handed in at Brinkley-cum-Snodsfield-in-the-
Marsh, it was signed "Travers," this revealing it as the
handiwork either of Aunt Dahlia or Thomas P. Travers, her
husband, a pleasant old bird whom she had married at her
second pop some years earlier. From the fact that it started
with the words "Bertie, you worm" I deduced that it was
the former who had taken post-office pen in hand. Uncle
Tom is more guarded in his speech than the female of the
species. He generally calls me "Me boy."

This was the substance of the communication:

BERTIE, YOU WORM, YOUR EARLY PRESENCE DESIRED. DROP
EVERYTHING AND COME DOWN HERE PRONTO, PREPARED
FOR LENGTHY VISIT. URGENTLY NEED YOU TO BUCK UP A
BLIGHTER WITH WHISKERS. LOVE. TRAVERS.

I brooded over this for the rest of the morning, and on
my way to lunch at the Drones shot off my answer, a brief
request for more light:

DID YOU SAY WHISKERS OR WHISKY? LOVE. WOOSTER.

I found another from her on returning:

WHISKERS, ASS. THE SON OF A WHAT-NOT HAS SHORT BUT
DISTINCT SIDE-WHISKERS. LOVE. TRAVERS.

It's an odd thing about memory, it so often just fails to
spear the desired object. At the back of my mind there
was dodging about a hazy impression that somewhere at
some time I heard someone mention short side-whiskers
in some connection, but I couldn't pin it down. It eluded
me. So, pursuing the sound old policy of going to the
fountainhead for information, I stepped out and dispatched the following:

WHAT SHORT-SIDE-WHISKERED SON OF A WHAT-NOT WOULD
THIS BE, AND WHY DOES HE NEED BUCKING UP? WIRE FULL
DETAILS, AS AT PRESENT FOGGED, BEWILDERED AND MYSTI-
FIED. LOVE. WOOSTER.

She replied with the generous warmth which causes so
many of her circle to hold on to their hats when she lets
herself go:

LISTEN, YOU FOUL BLOT. WHAT'S THE IDEA OF MAKING ME
SPEND A FORTUNE ON TELEGRAMS LIKE THIS? DO YOU
THINK I AM MADE OF MONEY? NEVER YOU MIND WHAT
SHORT-SIDE-WHISKERED SON OF A WHAT-NOT IT IS OR WHY
HE NEEDS BUCKING UP. YOU JUST COME AS I TELL YOU AND
LOOK SLIPPY ABOUT IT. OH, AND BY THE WAY, GO TO
ASPINALL'S IN BOND STREET AND GET PEARL NECKLACE OF
MINE THEY HAVE THERE AND BRING IT DOWN WITH YOU.

HAVE YOU GOT THAT? ASPINALL'S. BOND STREET. PEARL
NECKLACE. SHALL EXPECT YOU TOMORROW. LOVE. TRAVERS.

A little shaken but still keeping the flag flying, I
responded with the ensuing:

FULLY GRASP ALL THAT ASPINALL'S-BOND-STREET-PEARL-
NECKLACE STUFF, BUT WHAT YOU ARE OVERLOOKING IS THAT
COMING TO BRINKLEY AT PRESENT JUNCTURE NOT SO JOLLY
SIMPLE AS YOU SEEM TO THINK. THERE ARE COMPLICATIONS
AND WHAT NOT. WHEELS WITHIN WHEELS, IF YOU GET WHAT
I MEAN. WHOLE THING CALLS FOR DEEP THOUGHT. WILL
WEIGH MATTER CAREFULLY AND LET YOU KNOW DECISION.
LOVE. WOOSTER.

You see, though Brinkley Court is a home from home
and gets five stars in Baedeker as the headquarters of
Monsieur Anatole, Aunt Dahlia's French cook—a place,
in short, to which in ordinary circ. I race, when invited,
with a whoop and a holler, it had taken me but an instant
to spot that under existing conditions there were grave
objections to going there. I need scarcely say that I allude
to the fact that Florence was on the premises and Stilton
expected shortly.

It was this that was giving me pause. Who could say
that the latter, finding me in residence on his arrival,
would not leap to the conclusion that I had rolled up in
pursuit of the former like young Lochinvar coming out of
the west? And should this thought flit into his mind, what,
I asked myself, would the harvest be? His parting words
about my spine were still green in my memory. I knew
him to be a man rather careful in his speech, on whose
promises one could generally rely, and if he said he was

going to break spines in four places, you could be quite sure that four places was precisely what he would break them in.

I passed a restless and uneasy evening. In no mood for revelry at the Drones, I returned home early and was brushing up on my *Mystery of the Pink Crayfish* when the telephone rang, and so disordered was the nervous system that I shot ceilingwards at the sound. It was as much as I could do to totter across the room and unhook the receiver.

The voice that floated over the wire was that of Aunt Dahlia.

Well, when I say floated, possibly thundered would be more the *mot juste*. A girlhood and early womanhood spent in chivvying the British fox in all weathers under the auspices of the Quorn and Pytchley have left this aunt brick-red in color and lent amazing power to her vocal cords. I've never pursued foxes myself, but apparently, when you do, you put in a good bit of your time shouting across ploughed fields in a high wind, and this becomes a habit. If Aunt Dahlia has a fault, it is that she is inclined to talk to you when face to face in a small drawing-room as if she were addressing some crony a quarter of a mile away whom she had observed riding over hounds. For the rest, she is a large, jovial soul, built rather on the lines of Mae West, and is beloved by all including the undersigned. Our relations have always been chummy to the last drop.

"Hullo, hullo, hullo!" she boomed. The old hunting stuff coming to the surface, you notice. "Is that you, Bertie, darling?"

I said it was none other.

"Then what's the idea, you halfwitted Gadarene swine, of all this playing hard-to-get? You and your matter-weighing! I never heard such nonsense in my life. You've got to come here, and immediately, if you don't want an aunt's curse delivered on your doorstep by return of post. If I have to cope unaided with that ruddy Percy any longer, I shall crack beneath the strain."

She paused to take in breath, and I put a question.

"Is Percy the whiskered bloke?"

"That's the one. He's casting a thick pall of gloom over the place. It's like living in a fog. Tom says if something isn't done soon, he will take steps."

"But what's the matter with the chap?"

"He's madly in love with Florence Craye."

"Oh, I see. And it depresses him to think that she's engaged to Stilton Cheesewright?"

"Exactly. He's as sick as mud about it. He moons broodingly to and fro, looking like Hamlet. I want you to come and divert him. Take him for walks, dance before him, tell him funny stories. Anything to bring a smile to that whiskered, tortoiseshell-rimmed face."

I saw her point, of course. No hostess wants a Hamlet on the premises. But what I couldn't understand was how a chap like that came to be polluting the pure air of Brinkley. I knew the old relative to be quite choosey in the matter of guests. Cabinet ministers have sometimes failed to crash the gate. I put this to her, and she said the explanation was perfectly simple.

"I told you I was in the middle of a spot of business with Trotter. I've got the whole family here—Percy's stepfather, L. G. Trotter, Percy's mother, Mrs. Trotter, and Percy in person. I only wanted Trotter, but Mrs. T. and Percy rang themselves in."

"I see. What they call a package deal." I broke off, aghast. Memory had returned to its throne, and I knew now why that stuff about short side-whiskers had seemed to have a familiar ring. "Trotter?" I cried.

She whooped censoriously.

"Don't yell like that. You nearly broke my eardrum."

"But did you say Trotter?"

"Of course I said Trotter."

"This Percy's name isn't Gorringe?"

"That's what it unquestionably is. He admits it."

"Then I'm frightfully sorry, old thing, but I can't possibly come. It was only the other day that the above Gorringe was trying to nick me for a thousand quid to put into this play he's made of Florence's book, and I turned him down like a bedspread. You can readily see, then, how fraught with embarrassment a meeting in the flesh would be. I shouldn't know which way to look."

"If that's all that's worrying you, forget it. Florence tells me he has raised that thousand elsewhere."

"Well, I'm dashed. Where did he get it?"

"She doesn't know. He's secretive about it. He just said it was all right, he had got the stuff and they could go ahead. So you needn't be shy about meeting him. What if he does think you the world's premier louse? Don't we all?"

"Something in that."

"Then you'll come?"

I chewed the lower lip dubiously. I was thinking of Stilton.

"Well, speak, dumbbell," said the relative with asperity. "What's all the silence about?"

"I was musing."

"Then stop musing and give me the good word. If it will help to influence your decision, I may mention that Anatole is at the top of his form just now."

I started. If this was so, it would clearly be madness not to be one of the company ranged around the festive board.

I have touched so far only lightly on this Anatole, and I take the opportunity now of saying that his was an output which had to be tasted to be believed, mere words being inadequate to convey the full facts with regard to his amazing virtuosity. After one of Anatole's lunches has melted in the mouth, you unbutton the waistcoat and loll back, breathing heavily and feeling that life has no more to offer, and then, before you know where you are, along comes one of his dinners, with even more on the ball, the whole layout constituting something about as near Heaven as any reasonable man could wish.

I felt, accordingly, that no matter how vehemently Stilton might express and fulfill himself on discovering me . . . well, not perhaps exactly cheek by jowl with the woman he loved but certainly hovering in her vicinity, the risk of rousing the fiend within him was one that must be taken. It cannot ever, of course, be agreeable to find yourself torn into a thousand pieces with a fourteen-stone Othello doing a Shuffle off to Buffalo on the scattered fragments, but if you are full at the time of Anatole's *Timbale de ris de veau Toulousaine,* the discomfort unquestionably becomes modified.

"I'll come," I said.

"Good boy. With you taking Percy off my neck, I shall be free to concentrate on Trotter. And every ounce of concentration will be needed, if I'm to put this deal through."

"What is the deal? You never told me. Who is this Trotter, if any?"

"I met him at Agatha's. He's a friend of hers. He owns a lot of papers up in Liverpool and wants to establish a beachhead in London. So I'm trying to get him to buy a *Boudoir.*"

I was amazed. Absolutely the last thing I would have expected. I had always supposed *Milady's Boudoir* to be her ewe lamb. To learn that she contemplated selling it stunned me. It was like hearing that Rodgers had decided to sell Hammerstein.

"But why on earth? I thought you loved it like a son."

"I do, but the strain of having to keep going to Tom and trying to get money out of him for its support has got me down. Every time I start pleading with him for another check, he says 'But isn't it paying its way yet?' and I say 'No, darling, it is not paying its way yet,' and he says 'H'm!' adding that if this sort of thing goes on, we shall all be on the dole by next Christmas. It's become too much for me. It makes me feel like one of those women who lug babies around in the streets and want you to buy white heather. So when I met Trotter at Agatha's, I decided that he was the man who was going to take over, if human ingenuity could work it. What did you say?"

"I said 'Oh, ah.' I was about to add that it was a pity."

"Yes, quite a pity, but unavoidable. Tom gets more difficult to touch daily. He says he loves me dearly, but enough is sufficient. Well, I'll expect you tomorrow, then. Don't forget the necklace."

"I'll send Jeeves over for it in the morning."

"Right."

I think she would have spoken further, but at this moment a female voice off stage said "Three-ee-ee minutes," and she hung up with the sharp cry of a woman who fears she is going to be soaked for another couple of bob or whatever it is.

Jeeves came trickling in.

"Oh, Jeeves," I said, "we shall be heading for Brinkley tomorrow."

"Very good, sir."

"Aunt Dahlia wants me there to infuse a bit of the party spirit into our old pal Percy Gorringe, who is at the moment infesting the joint."

"Indeed, sir? I wonder, sir, if it would be possible for you to allow me to return to London next week for the afternoon?"

"Certainly, Jeeves, certainly. You have some beano in prospect?"

"It is the monthly luncheon of the Junior Ganymede Club, sir. I have been asked to take the chair."

"Take it by all means, Jeeves. A well-deserved honor."

"Thank you, sir. I shall of course return the same day."

"You'll make a speech, no doubt?"

"Yes, sir. A speech from the chair is of the essence."

"I'll bet you have them rolling in the aisles. Oh, Jeeves, I was nearly forgetting. Aunt Dahlia wants me to bring her necklace. It's at Aspinall's in Bond Street. Will you toddle over and get it in the morning?"

"Certainly, sir."

"And another thing I almost forgot to mention. Percy has raised that thousand quid."

"Indeed, sir?"

"He must have approached someone with a more bite-able ear than mine. One wonders who the mug was."

"Yes, sir."

"Some halfwit, one presumes."

"No doubt, sir."

"Still, there it is. It just bears out what the late Barnum used to say about there being one born every minute."

"Precisely, sir. Would that be all, sir?"

"Yes, that's all. Good night, Jeeves."

"Good night, sir. I will attend to the packing in the morning."

9

IT WAS GETTING on for the quiet evenfall on the morrow when after a pleasant drive through the smiling countryside I steered the two-seater in at the gates of Brinkley Court and ankled along to inform my hostess that I had come aboard. I found her in her snuggery or den, taking it easy with a cup of tea and an Agatha Christie. As I presented myself, she gave the moustache a swift glance, but apart from starting like a nymph surprised while bathing and muttering something about "Was this the face that stopped a thousand clocks?" made no comment. One received the impression that she was saving it up.

"Hullo, reptile," she said. "You're here, are you?"

"Here I am," I responded, "with my hair in a braid and ready to the last button. A very merry Pip-pip to you, aged relative."

"The same to you, fathead. I suppose you forgot to bring that necklace?"

"Far from it. Here it is. It's the one Uncle Tom gave you at Christmas, isn't it?"

"That's right. He likes to see me wearing it at dinner."

"As who wouldn't?" I said courteously. I handed it over and helped myself to a slice of buttered toast. "Well, nice to be in the old home once more. I'm in my usual room, I take it? And how is everything in and around Brinkley Court? Anatole all right?"

"Never better."

"You look pretty roguish."

"Oh, I'm fine."

"And Uncle Tom?"

A cloud passed over her shining evening face.

"Tom's still a bit low, poor old buster."

"Owing to Percy, you mean?"

"That's right."

"There has been no change then in this Gorringe's gloom?"

"Naturally not. He's been worse than ever since Florence got here. Tom winces every time he sees him, especially at meals. He says that having to watch Percy push away untasted food cooked by Anatole gives him a rush of blood to the head, and that gives him indigestion. You know how sensitive his stomach is."

I patted her hand.

"Be of good cheer," I said. "I'll buck Perce up. Freddie Widgeon was showing me a trick with two corks and a bit of string the other night which cannot fail to bring a smile to the most tortured face. It had the lads at the Drones in stitches. You will doubtless be able to provide a couple of corks?"

"Twenty, if you wish."

"Good." I took a cake with pink icing on it. "So much for Percy. What of the rest of the personnel? Anybody here besides the Trotter gang and Florence?"

"Not yet. Tom said something about somebody named Lord Sidcup looking in for dinner tomorrow on his way to the brine baths at Droitwich. Do you know him?"

"Never heard of him. He's a sealed book to me."

"He's some man Tom met in London. Apparently he's a bit of a nib on old silver, and Tom wants to show him his collection."

I nodded. I knew this uncle to be greatly addicted to the collecting of old silver. His apartments both at Brinkley Court and at his house in Charles Street are full of things I wouldn't be seen dead in a ditch with.

"What they call a virtuoso this Lord Sidcup would be, I presume?"

"Something on those lines."

"Ah well, it takes all sorts to make a world, does it not?"

"We shall also have with us tomorrow the boy friend Cheesewright, and the day after that Daphne Dolores Morehead. She's the novelist."

"I know. Florence was telling me about her. You've bought a serial from her, I understand."

"Yes. I thought it would be a shrewd move to salt the mine."

I didn't get this. She seemed to me an aunt who was talking in riddles.

"How do you mean, salt the mine? What mine? This is the first I've heard of any mines."

I think that if her mouth had not been full of buttered toast, she would have clicked her tongue, for as soon as she had cleared the gangway with a quick swallow she spoke impatiently, as if my slowness in the uptake had exasperated her.

"You really are an abysmal ass, young Bertie. Haven't you ever heard of salting mines? It's a recognized business precaution. When you've got a dud mine you want to sell to a mug, you sprinkle an ounce or two of gold over it and summon the mug to come along and inspect the property. He rolls up, sees the gold, feels that this is what the doctor ordered and reaches for his check book. I worked on the same principle."

I was still at a loss, and said so, and this time she did click her tongue.

"Can't you grasp it, chump? I bought the serial to make the paper look good to Trotter. He sees the announcement that a Daphne Morehead opus is coming along and is terrifically impressed. 'Gosh!' he says to himself. 'Daphne Dolores Morehead and everything! *Milady's Boudoir* must be hot stuff.'"

"But don't these blokes want to see books and figures and things before they brass up?"

"Not if they've been having Anatole's cooking for a week or more. That's why I asked him down here."

I saw what she meant, and her reasoning struck me as sound. There is something about those lunches and dinners of Anatole's that mellows you and saps your cool judgment. After tucking into them all this time I presumed that L. G. Trotter was going about in a sort of rosy mist, wanting to do kind acts right and left like a Boy Scout. Continue the treatment a few more days, and he would probably beg her as a personal favor to accept twice what she was asking.

"Very shrewd," I said. "Yes, I think you're on the right lines. Has Anatole been giving you his *Rognons aux Montagnes?*"

"*And his Selle d'Agneau aux laitues à la Grecque.*"

"Then I would say the thing was in the bag. All over but the cheering. But here's a point that has been puzzling me," I said. "Florence tells me that La Morehead is one of the more costly of our female pen-pushers and has to have purses of gold flung to her in great profusion before she will consent to sign on the dotted line. Correct?"

"Quite correct."

"Then how the dickens," I said, getting down to it in my keen way, "did you contrive to extract the necessary ore from Uncle Tom? Didn't he pay his income tax this year?"

"You bet he did. I should have thought you would have heard his screams in London. Poor old boy, how he does suffer on these occasions."

She spoke sooth. Uncle Tom, though abundantly provided with the chips, having been until his retirement one of those merchant princes who scoop it up in sackfuls out East, has a rooted objection to letting the hellbounds of the Inland Revenue dip in and get theirs. For weeks after they have separated him from his hard-earned he is inclined to go off into corners and sit with his head between his hands, muttering about ruin and the sinister trend of socialistic legislation and what is to become of us all if this continues.

"He certainly does," I assented. "Quite the soul in torment, what? And yet, despite this, you succeeded in nicking him for what must have been a small fortune. How did you do it? From what you were saying on the phone last night I got the impression that he was in more than usually non-parting mood these days. You conjured up in my mind's eye the picture of a man who was sticking his ears back and refusing to play ball, like Balaam's ass."

"What do you know about Balaam's ass?"

"Me? I know Balaam's ass from soup to nuts. Have you forgotten that when a pupil at the Rev. Aubrey Upjohn's educational establishment at Bramley-on-Sea I once won a prize for Scripture Knowledge?"

"I'll bet you cribbed."

"Not at all. My triumph was due to sheer merit. But, getting back to it, how did you induce Uncle Tom to scare the moths from his pocketbook? It must have required quite a scuttleful of wifely wiles on your part?"

I wouldn't like to say of a loved aunt that she giggled, but unquestionably the sound that proceeded from her lips closely resembled a giggle.

"Oh, I managed."

"But how?"

"Never mind how, you pestilential young Nosey Parker. I managed."

"I see," I said, letting it go. Something told me she did not wish to spill the data. "And how is the Trotter deal coming along?"

I seemed to have touched an exposed nerve. The giggle died on her lips, and her face—always, as I have said, on the reddish side—deepened in color to a rich mauve.

"Blister his blighted insides!" she said, speaking with the explosive heat which had once made fellow-members of the Quorn and Pytchley leap convulsively in their saddles. "I don't know what's the matter with the son of Belial. Here he is, with nine of Anatole's lunches and eight of Anatole's dinners tucked away among the gastric juices, and he refuses to get down to brass tacks. He hums—"

"What on earth does he do that for?"

"—and haws. He evades the issue. I strain every nerve to make him talk turkey, but I can't pin him down. He doesn't say Yes and he doesn't say No."

"There's a song called that . . . or, rather, 'She Didn't Say Yes and She Didn't Say No.' I sing it a good deal in my bath. It goes like this."

I started to render the refrain in a pleasant light baritone, but desisted on receiving Agatha Christie abaft the frontal bone. The old relative seemed to have fired from the hip like somebody in a Western B picture.

"Don't try me too high, Bertie dear," she said gently, and fell into what looked like a reverie. "Do you know what I think is the trouble?" she went on, coming out of it. "I believe Ma Trotter is responsible for this non-cooperation of his. For some reason she doesn't want him to put the deal through, and has told him he mustn't. It's the only explanation I can think of. When I met him at Agatha's, he spoke as if it were just a matter of arranging terms, but these last few days he has come over all coy, as if acting under orders from up top. When you stood them dinner that night, did he strike you as being crushed beneath her heel?"

"Very much so. He wept with delight when she gave him a smile and trembled with fear at her frown. But why would she object to him buying the *Boudoir*?"

"Don't ask me. It's a complete mystery."

"You haven't put her back up somehow since she got here?"

"Certainly not. I've been fascinating."

"And yet there it is, what?"

"Exactly. There it blasted well is, curse it."

I heaved a sympathetic sigh. Mine is a tender heart, easily wrung, and the spectacle of this good old egg mourning over what might have been had wrung it like a ton of bricks.

"Too bad," I said. "One had hoped for better things."

"One had," she assented. "I was so sure that Morehead serial would have brought home the bacon."

"Of course, he may be just thinking it over."

"That's true."

"A fellow thinking it over would naturally hum."

"And haw?"

"And, possibly, also haw. You could scarcely expect him to do less."

We would no doubt have proceeded to go more deeply into the matter, subjecting this humming and hawing of L. G. Trotter's to a close analysis, but at this moment the door opened and a careworn face peered in, a face disfigured on either side by short whiskers and in the middle by tortoiseshell-rimmed spectacles.

"I say," said the face, contorted with anguish, "have you seen Florence?"

Aunt Dahlia replied that she had not been privileged to do so since lunch.

"I thought she might be with you."

"She isn't."

"Oh," said the face, still running the gamut of the emotions, and began to recede.

"Hey!" cried Aunt Dahlia, arresting it as it was about to disappear. She went to the desk and picked up a buff envelope. "This telegram came for her just now. Will you give it to her if you see her. And while you're here, meet my nephew Bertie Wooster, the pride of Piccadilly."

Well, I hadn't expected him on learning of my identity to dance about the room on the tips of his toes, and he didn't. He gave me a long, reproachful look, similar in its essentials to that which a black beetle gives a cook when the latter is sprinkling insect powder on it.

"I have corresponded with Mr. Wooster," he said coldly. "We have also spoken on the telephone."

He turned and was gone, gazing at me reproachfully to the last. It was plain that the Gorringes did not lightly forget.

"That was Percy," said Aunt Dahlia.

I replied that I had divined as much.

"Did you notice how he looked when he said 'Florence'? Like a dying duck in a thunderstorm."

"And did you notice," I inquired in my turn, "how he looked when you said 'Bertie Wooster'? Like someone finding a dead mouse in his pint of beer. Not a bonhommous bird. Not my type."

"No. You would scarcely suppose that even a mother could view him without nausea, would you? And yet he is the apple of Ma Trotter's eye. She loves him as much as she hates Mrs. Alderman Blenkinsop. Did she touch on Mrs. Alderman Blenkinsop at that dinner of yours?"

"At several points during the meal. Who is she?"

"Her bitterest social rival up in Liverpool."

"Do they have social rivals up in Liverpool?"

"You bet they do, in droves. I gather that it is nip and tuck between the Trotter and the Blenkinsop as to who shall be the uncrowned queen of Liverpudlian society. Sometimes one gets her nose in front, sometimes the other. It's like what one used to read about the death struggles for supremacy in New York's Four Hundred in the old days. But why am I telling you all this? You ought to be out there in the sunset, racing after Percy and bucking him up with your off-color stories. You have a fund of off-color stories, I presume?"

"Oh, rather."

"Then get going, laddie. Once more unto the breach, dear friends, once more, or close the wall up with our English dead. Yoicks! Tally-ho! Hark for'ard!" she added, reverting to the argot of the hunting field.

Well, when Aunt Dahlia tells you to get going, you get going, if you know what's good for you. But I was in no cheery mood as I made my way into the great open spaces. That look of Percy's had told me he was going to be a hard audience. It had had in it much of the austerity which I had noticed in Stilton Cheesewright's Uncle Joseph during our get-together at Vinton Street police court.

It was with not a little satisfaction, accordingly, that I found on arriving in the open no signs of him. Relieved, I abandoned the chase and started to stroll hither and thither, taking the air. And I hadn't taken much of it, when there he was, rounding a rhododendron bush in my very path.

10

IF IT HADN'T BEEN for the whiskers, I don't believe I would have recognized him. It was only about ten minutes since he had shoved his face in at the door of Aunt Dahlia's lair, but in that brief interval his whole aspect had changed. No longer the downcast duck in a thunderstorm from whom I had so recently parted, he had become gay and bobbish. His air was jaunty, his smile bright, and there was in his demeanor more than a suggestion of a man who might at any moment break into a tap dance. It was as if he had spent a considerable time watching that trick of Freddie Widgeon's with the two corks and the bit of string.

"Hullo there, Wooster," he cried buoyantly, and you would have supposed that finding Bertram in his midst had just about made his day. "Taking a stroll, eh?"

I said Yes, I was taking a stroll, and he beamed as though feeling that I could have pursued no wiser and more admirable course. *Sensible chap, Wooster*, he seemed to be saying. *He takes strolls.*

There was a short intermission here, during which he looked at me lovingly and slid his feet about a bit in the manner of one trying out dance steps. Then he said it was a beautiful evening, and I endorsed this.

"The sunset," he said, indicating it.

"Very fruity," I agreed, for the whole horizon was aflame with glorious technicolor.

"Seeing it," he said, "I am reminded of a poem I wrote the other day for *Parnassus*. Just a little thing I dashed off. You might care to hear it."

"Oh, rather."

"It's called 'Caliban at Sunset.'"

"What at sunset?"

"Caliban."

He cleared his throat, and began:

> *I stood with a man*
> *Watching the sun go down.*
> *The air was full of murmurous summer scents*
> *And a brave breeze sang like a bugle*
> *From a sky that smoldered in the west,*
> *A sky of crimson, amethyst and gold and sepia*
> *And blue as blue as were the eyes of Helen*
> *When she sat*
> *Gazing from some high tower in Ilium*
> *Upon the Grecian tents darkling below.*
> *And he,*
> *This man who stood beside me,*
> *Gaped like some dull, halfwitted animal*
> *And said,*
> *"I say,*
> *Doesn't that sunset remind you*
> *Of a slice*
> *Of underdone roast beef?"*

He opened his eyes, which he had closed in order to render the *morceau* more effectively.

"Bitter, of course."

"Oh, frightfully bitter."

"I was feeling bitter when I wrote it. I think you know a man named Cheesewright. It was he I had in mind. Actually, we had never stood watching a sunset together, but I felt it was just the sort of thing he would have said if he had been watching a sunset, if you see what I mean. Am I right?"

"Quite right."

"A soulless clod, don't you think?"

"Soulless to the core."

"No finer feelings?"

"None."

"Would I be correct in describing him as a pumpkin-headed oaf?"

"Quite correct."

"Yes," he said, "she is well out of it."

"She?"

"Florence."

"Oh, ah. Well out of what?"

He eyed me speculatively, heaving gently like a saucepan of porridge about to reach the height of its fever. I am a man who can observe and deduce, and it was plain to me, watching him sizzle, that something had happened pretty recently in his affairs which had churned him up like a seidlitz powder, leaving him with but two alternatives—(a) to burst where he stood and (b) to decant his pent-up emotions on the first human being who came along. No doubt he would have preferred this human being to have been of a non-Wooster nature, but one imagines that he was saying to himself that you can't have everything and that he was in no position to pick and choose.

He decided on Alternative B.

"Wooster," he said, placing a hand on my shoulder, "may I ask you a question? Has your aunt told you that I love Florence Craye?"

"She did mention it, yes."

"I thought she might have done. She is not what I would call a reticent woman, though of course with many excellent qualities. I was forced to take her into my confidence soon after my arrival here, because she asked me why the devil I was going about looking like a dead codfish."

"Or like Hamlet?"

"Hamlet or a dead codfish. The point is immaterial. I confessed to her that it was because I loved Florence with a consuming passion and had discovered that she was engaged to the oaf Cheesewright. It had been, I explained, as if I had received a crushing blow on the head."

"Like Sir Eustace Willoughby."

"I beg your pardon?"

"In *The Mystery of the Pink Crayfish.* He was conked on the bean in his library one night, and if you ask me it was the butler who did it. But I interrupted you."

"You did."

"I'm sorry. You were saying it was as if you had received a crushing blow on the head."

"Exactly. I reeled beneath the shock."

"Must have been a nasty jar."

"It was. I was stunned. But now . . . You remember that telegram your aunt gave me to give to Florence?"

"Ah, yes, the telegram."

"It was from Cheesewright, breaking the engagement."

I had no means of knowing, of course, what his form was when reeling beneath shocks, but I doubted whether he could have put up a performance topping mine as I heard these words. The sunset swayed before my eyes as if it were doing the shimmy, and a bird close by which was getting outside its evening worm looked for an instant like two birds, both flickering.

"What!" I gurgled, rocking on my base.

"Yes."

"He's broken the engagement?"

"Precisely."

"Oh, golly! Why?"

He shook his head.

"Ah, that I couldn't tell you. All I know is that I found Florence in the stable yard tickling a cat behind the ear, and I came up and said 'Here's a telegram for you,' and she said 'Really? I suppose it's from D'Arcy.' I shuddered at the name, and while I was shuddering, she opened the envelope. It was a long telegram, but she had not read more than the first words when she uttered a sharp cry. 'Bad news?' I queried. Her eyes flashed, and a cold, proud look came into her face. 'Not at all,' she replied. 'Splendid news. D'Arcy Cheesewright has broken the engagement.'"

"Gosh!"

"You may well say 'Gosh!'"

"She didn't tell you any more than that?"

"No. She said one or two incisive things about Cheesewright with which I thoroughly concurred and strode off in the direction of the kitchen garden. And I came away, walking, as you may well imagine, on air. I deprecate the modern tendency to use slang, but I am not ashamed to confess that what I was saying to myself was the word 'Whoopee!' Excuse me, Wooster, I must now leave you. I can't keep still."

And with these words he pranced off like a mustang, leaving me to face the changed conditions alone.

It was with a brooding sense of peril that I did so. And if

you are saying "But why, Wooster? Surely everything is pretty smooth? What matter if the girl's nuptials with Cheesewright have been canceled, when here is Percy Gorringe all ready and eager to take up the white man's burden?" I reply "Ah, but you've not seen Percy Gorringe." I mean to say, I couldn't picture Florence, however much on the rebound, accepting the addresses of a man who voluntarily wore side-whiskers and wrote poems about sunsets. Far more likely, it seemed to me, that having a vacant date on her hands she would once again reach out for the old and tried—viz. poor old Bertram. It was what she had done before, and these things tend to become a habit.

I was completely at a loss to imagine what could have caused this in-and-out running on Stilton's part. The thing didn't make sense. When last seen, it will be remembered, he had had all the earmarks of one about whom Love had twined its silken fetters. His every word at that parting chat of ours had indicated this beyond peradventure and doubt. Dash it, I mean, you don't go telling people you will break their spines in four places if they come oiling round the adored object unless you have more than a passing fancy for the bally girl.

So what had occurred to dim the lamp of love and all that sort of thing?

Could it be, I asked myself, that the strain of growing that moustache had proved too much for him? Had he caught sight of himself in the mirror about the third day— the third day is always the danger spot—and felt that nothing in the way of wedded bliss could make the venture worth while? Called upon to choose between the woman he loved and a hairless upper lip, had he cracked, with the result that the lip had had it by a landslide?

With a view to getting the inside stuff straight from the

horse's mouth, I hurried to the kitchen garden, where, if Percy was to be relied on, Florence would now be, probably pacing up and down with lowered head.

She was there with lowered head, though not actually pacing up and down. She was bending over a gooseberry bush, eating gooseberries in an overwrought sort of way. Seeing me, she straightened up, and I snapped into the *res* without preamble.

"What's all this I hear from Percy Gorringe?" I said.

She swallowed a gooseberry with a passionate gulp that spoke eloquently of the churned-up soul, and I saw, as Percy's words had led me to expect, that she was madder than a wet hen. Her whole aspect was that of a girl who would have given her year's dress allowance for the privilege of beating G. D'Arcy Cheesewright over the head with a parasol.

I continued.

"He says there has been a rift within the lute."

"I beg your pardon?"

"You and Stilton. According to Percy, the lute is not the lute it was. Stilton has broken the engagement, he tells me."

"He has. I'm delighted, of course."

"Delighted? You like the setup?"

"Of course I do. What girl would not be delighted who finds herself unexpectedly free from a man with a pink face and a head that looks as if it had been blown up with a bicycle pump?"

I clutched the brow. I am a pretty astute chap, and I could see that this was not the language of love. I mean, if you had heard Juliet saying a thing like that about Romeo, you would have raised the eyebrows in quick concern, wondering if all was well with the young couple.

"But when I saw him last, everything seemed perfectly

okey-doke. I could have sworn that, however reluctantly, he had reconciled himself to growing that moustache."

She stooped and took another gooseberry.

"It has nothing to do with moustaches," she said, reappearing on the surface. "The whole thing is due to the fact that D'Arcy Cheesewright is a low, mean, creeping, crawling, slinking, spying, despicable worm," she proceeded, dishing out the words from between clenched teeth. "Do you know what he did?"

"I haven't a notion."

She refreshed herself with a further gooseberry and returned to the upper air, breathing a few puffs of flame through the nostrils.

"He sneaked round to that night club yesterday and made inquiries."

"Oh, my gosh!"

"Yes. You wouldn't think a man could stoop so low, but he bribed people and was allowed to look at the head waiter's book and found that a table had been reserved that night in your name. This confirmed his degraded suspicions. He knew that I had been there with you. I suppose," said Florence, diving at the gooseberry bush once more and starting to strip it of its contents, "a man gets a rotten, spying mind like that from being a policeman."

To say that I was appalled would not be putting it any too strongly. I was, moreover, astounded. It was a revelation to me that a puff-faced poop like Stilton could have been capable of detective work on this uncanny scale. I had always respected his physique, of course, but had supposed that the ability to fell an ox with a single blow more or less let him out. Not for an instant had I credited him with reasoning powers which might well have made Hercule Poirot himself draw the breath in with a startled

"What ho." It just showed how one ought never to under-estimate a man simply because he devotes his life to shoving oars into rivers and pulling them out again, this being about as silly a way of passing the time as could be hit upon.

No doubt, as Florence had said, this totally unforeseen snakiness was the result of his having been, if only briefly, a member of the police force. One presumes that when the neophyte has been issued his uniform and regulation boots, the men up top take him aside and teach him a few things likely to be of use to him in his chosen profession. Stilton, it was plain, had learned his lesson well and, if one did but know, was probably capable of measuring blood stains and collecting cigar ash.

However, it was only fleeting attention that I gave to this facet of the situation. My thoughts were concentrated on something of far greater pith and moment, as Jeeves would say. I allude to the position—now that the man knew all—of B. Wooster, which seemed to me sticky to a degree. Florence, having sated herself with gooseberries, was starting to move off, and I arrested her with a sharp "Hoy!"

"That telegram," I said.

"I don't want to talk about it."

"I do. Was there anything about me in it?"

"Oh, yes, quite a lot."

I swallowed a couple of times and passed a finger round the inside of my collar. I had thought there might be.

"Did he hint at any plans he had with regard to me?"

"He said he was going to break your spine in five places."

"*Five* places?"

"I think he said five. Don't you let him," said Florence warmly, and it was nice, of course, to know that she disapproved. "Breaking spines! I never heard of such a thing. He ought to be ashamed of himself."

And she moved off in the direction of the house, walking like a tragedy queen on one of her bad mornings.

What I have heard Jeeves call the glimmering landscape was now fading on the sight, and it was getting on for the hour when dressing-gongs are beaten. But though I knew how rash it is ever to be late for one of Anatole's dinners, I could not bring myself to go in and don the soup-and-fish. I had so much to occupy the mind that I lingered on in a sort of stupor. Winged creatures of the night kept rolling up and taking a look at me and rolling off again, but I remained motionless, plunged in thought. A man pursued by a thug like D'Arcy Cheesewright has need of all the thought he can get hold of.

And then, quite suddenly, out of the night that covered me, black as the pit from pole to pole, there shone a gleam of light. It spread, illuminating the entire horizon, and I realized that, taken by and large, I was sitting pretty.

You see, what I had failed till now to spot was the fact that Stilton hadn't a notion that I was at Brinkley. Thinking me to be in the metropolis, it was there that he would be spreading his dragnet. He would call at the flat, ring bells, get no answer and withdraw, baffled. He would haunt the Drones, expecting me to drop in, and eventually, when I didn't so drop, would slink away, baffled again. "He cometh not," he would say, no doubt grinding his teeth, and a fat lot of good that would do him.

And of course, after what had occurred, there was no chance of him visiting Brinkley. A man who has broken off his engagement doesn't go to the country house where he knows the girl to be. Well, I mean, I ask you. Naturally he doesn't. If there was one spot on earth which could be counted on as of even date to be wholly free from Cheese-wrights, it was Brinkley Court, Brinkley-cum-Snodsfield-in-the-Marsh, Worcestershire.

Profoundly relieved, I picked up the feet and hastened to my room with a song on my lips. Jeeves was there, not actually holding a stop watch but obviously shaking his head a bit over the young master's tardiness. His left eyebrow quivered perceptibly as I entered.

"Yes, I know I'm late, Jeeves," I said, starting to shed the upholstery. "I went for a stroll."

He accepted the explanation indulgently.

"I quite understand, sir. It had occurred to me that, the evening being so fine, you were probably enjoying a saunter in the grounds. I told Mr. Cheesewright that this was no doubt the reason for your absence."

11

HALF IN AND HALF OUT of the shirt, I froze like one of those fellows in the old fairy stories who used to talk out of turn to magicians and have spells cast upon them. My ears were sticking up like a wirehaired terrier's, and I could scarcely believe that they had heard aright.

"Mr. Church?" I quavered. "What's that, Jeeves?"

"Sir?"

"I don't understand you. Are you saying . . . are you telling me . . . are you actually asserting that Stilton Cheesewright is on the premises?"

"Yes, sir. He arrived not long ago in his car. I found him waiting here. He expressed a desire to see you and appeared chagrined at your continued absence. Eventually, the dinner hour becoming imminent, he took his departure. He is hoping, I gathered from his remarks, to establish contact with you at the conclusion of the meal."

I slid dumbly into the shirt and started to tie the tie. I was quivering, partly with apprehension but even more with justifiable indignation. To say that I felt that this was a bit thick would not be straining the facts unduly. I mean, I knew D'Arcy Cheesewright to be of coarse fiber, the sort of bozo who, as Percy had said, would look at a sunset and see in it only a resemblance to a slice of underdone roast beef, but surely one is entitled to expect even bozos of coarse fiber to have a certain amount of delicacy and decent feeling and what not. This breaking off his engagement to Florence with one hand and coming thrusting his society on her with the other struck me, as it would have struck any fineminded man, as about as near the outside rim as it was possible to go.

"It's monstrous, Jeeves!" I cried. "Has this pumpkin-headed oaf no sense of what is fitting? Has he no tact, no discretion? Are you aware that this very evening, through the medium of a telegram which I have every reason to believe was a stinker, he severed his relations with Lady Florence?"

"No, sir, I had not been apprised. Mr. Cheesewright did not confide in me."

"He must have stopped off en route to compose the communication for it arrived not so very long before he did. Fancy doing the thing by telegram, thus giving some post-office clerk the laugh of a lifetime. And then actually having the crust to come barging in here! That, Jeeves, is serving it up with cream sauce. I don't want to be harsh, but there is only one word for D'Arcy Cheesewright—the word 'uncouth.' What are you goggling at?" I asked, noticing that his gaze was fixed upon me in a meaning manner.

He spoke with quiet severity.

"Your tie, sir. It will not, I fear, pass muster."

"Is this a time to talk of ties?"

"Yes, sir. One aims at the perfect butterfly shape, and this you have not achieved. With your permission, I will adjust it."

He did so, and I must say made a very fine job of it, but I continued to chafe.

"Do you realize, Jeeves, that my life is in peril?"

"Indeed, sir?"

"I assure you. That hunk of boloney . . . I allude to G. D'Arcy Cheesewright . . . has formally stated his intention of breaking my spine in five places."

"Indeed, sir? Why is that?"

I gave him the facts, and he expressed his opinion that the position of affairs was disturbing.

I shot one of my looks at him.

"You would go so far as that, Jeeves?"

"Yes, sir. Most disturbing."

"Ho!" I said, borrowing a bit of Stilton's stuff, and was about to tell him that if he couldn't think of a better word than that to describe what was probably the ghastliest imbroglio that had ever broken loose in the history of the human race, I would be glad to provide him with a Roget's *Thesaurus* at my personal expense, when the gong went and I had to leg it for the trough.

I do not look back to that first dinner at Brinkley Court as among the pleasantest functions which I have attended. Ironically, considering the circumstances, Anatole, that wizard of the pots and pans, had come through with one of his supremest efforts. He had provided the company with, if memory serves me correctly,

> *Le Caviar Frais*
> *Le Consommé aux Pommes d'Amour*
> *Les Sylphides à la crème d'Ecrevisses*
> *Les Fried Smelts*
> *Le Bird of some kind with chipped potatoes*
> *Le Ice Cream*

and, of course, *les fruits* and *le café*, but for all its effect on the Wooster soul it might have been corned beef hash. I don't say I pushed it away untasted, as Aunt Dahlia had described Percy doing with his daily ration, but the successive courses turned to ashes in my mouth. The sight of Stilton across the table blunted appetite.

I suppose it was just imagination, but he seemed to have grown quite a good deal both upwards and sideways since I had last seen him, and the play of expression on his salmon-colored face showed only too clearly the thoughts that were occupying his mind, if you could call it that. He gave me from eight to ten dirty looks in the course of the meal, but except for a remark at the outset to the effect that he was hoping to have a word with me later, did not address me.

Nor, for the matter of that, did he address anyone. His demeanor throughout was that of a homicidal deaf mute. The Trotter female, who sat on his right, endeavored to entertain him with a saga about Mrs. Alderman Blenkinsop's questionable behavior at a recent church bazaar, but he confined his response to gaping at her like some dull, halfwitted animal, as Percy would have said, and digging silently into the foodstuffs.

Sitting next to Florence, who spoke little, merely looking cold and proud and making bread pills, I had ample leisure for thought during the festivities, and by the time the coffee came round I had formed my plans and perfected my strategy. When eventually Aunt Dahlia blew the whistle for the gentler sex to buzz off and leave the men to their port, I took advantage of their departure to execute a quiet sneak through the french windows into the garden, being well in the open before the first of the procession had crossed the threshold. Whether or not this clever move brought a hoarse cry to Stilton's lips, I cannot say for certain, but I fancied I heard something that sounded like the howl of a timber wolf that has stubbed its toe on a passing rock. Not bothering to go back and ask if he had spoken, I made my way into the spacious grounds.

Had circumstances been different from what they were—not, of course, that they ever are—I might have derived no little enjoyment from this after-dinner saunter, for the air was full of murmurous summer scents and a brave breeze sang like a bugle from a sky liberally studded with stars. But to appreciate a starlit garden one has to have a fairly tranquil mind, and mine was about as far from being tranquil as it could jolly well stick.

What to do? I was asking myself. It seemed to me that the prudent course, if I wished to preserve a valued spine intact, would be to climb aboard the two-seater first thing in the morning and ho for the open spaces. To remain in statu quo would, it was clear, involve a distasteful nippiness on my part, for only by the most unremitting activity could I hope to elude Stilton and foil his sinister aims. I would be compelled, I saw, to spend a substantial portion of my time flying like a youthful hart or roe over the hills where spices grow, as I remembered having heard Jeeves once put it, and the Woosters resent having to sink to the level of harts and roes, whether juvenile or getting on in years. We have our pride.

I had just reached the decision that on the morrow I would melt away like snow on the mountain tops and go to America or Australia or the Fiji Islands or somewhere for awhile, when the murmurous summer scents were augmented by the aroma of a powerful cigar and I observed a dim figure approaching. After a tense moment when I supposed it to be Stilton and braced myself for a spot of that youthful-hart-or-roe stuff, I got it placed. It was only Uncle Tom, taking his nightly prowl.

Uncle Tom is a great lad for prowling in the garden. A man with grayish hair and a face like a walnut—not that that has anything to do with it, of course—I just mention it in passing—he likes to be among the shrubs and flowers early and late, particularly late, for he suffers a bit from insomnia and the tribal medicine man told him that a breath of fresh air before hitting the hay would bring relief.

Seeing me, he paused for station identification.

"Is that you, Bertie, me boy?"

I conceded this, and he hove alongside, puffing smoke.

"Why did you leave us?" he asked, alluding to that quick duck of mine from the dining-room.

"Oh, I thought I would."

"Well, you didn't miss much. What a set! That man Trotter makes me sick."

"Oh, yes?"

"His stepson Percy makes me sick."

"Oh, yes?"

"And that fellow Cheesewright makes me sick. They all make me sick," said Uncle Tom. He is not one of your jolly-innkeeper-with-entrance-number-in-act-one hosts. He looks with ill-concealed aversion on at least ninety-four per cent of the guests within his gates and spends most of his time dodging them. "Who invited Cheesewright here? Dahlia, I suppose, though why we shall never know. A deleterious young slab of damnation, if ever I saw one. But she will do these things. I've even known her to invite her sister Agatha. Talking of Dahlia, Bertie, me boy, I'm worried about her."

"Worried?"

"Exceedingly worried. I believe she's sickening for something. Has her manner struck you as strange since you got here?"

I mused.

"No, I don't think so," I said. "She seemed to be about the same as usual. How do you mean, strange?"

He waved a concerned cigar. He and the old relative are a fond and united couple.

"It was just now, when I looked in on her in her room to ask if she would care to come for a stroll. She said No, she didn't think she would, because if she went out at night she always swallowed moths and midges and things and she didn't believe it was good for her on top of a heavy dinner. And we were talking idly of this and that, when she suddenly seemed to come all over faint."

"Swooned, do you mean?"

"No, I wouldn't say she actually swooned. She continued perpendicular. But she tottered, pressing her hand to the top of her head. Pale as a ghost she looked."

"Odd."

"Very. It worried me. I'm not at all easy in my mind about her."

I pondered.

"It couldn't have been something you said that upset her?"

"Impossible. I was talking about this fellow Sidcup who's coming tomorrow to look at my silver collection. You've never met him, have you?"

"No."

"Rather a fatheaded ass," said Uncle Tom, who thinks most of his circle fatheaded asses, "but apparently knows quite a bit about old silver and jewelry and all that sort of thing, and anyway he'll only be here for dinner, thank

God," he added in his hospitable way. "But I was telling you about your aunt. As I was saying, she tottered and looked as pale as a ghost. The fact of the matter is, she's been overdoing it. This paper of hers, this *Madame's Nightshirt* or whatever it's called. It's wearing her to a shadow. Silly nonsense. What does she want with a weekly paper? I'll be thankful if she sells it to this man Trotter and gets rid of the damned thing, because apart from wearing her to a shadow it's costing me a fortune. Money, money, money, there's no end to it."

He then spoke with considerable fervor for awhile of income tax and surtax, and after making a tentative appointment to meet me in the breadline at an early date popped off and was lost in the night. And I, feeling that, the hour being now advanced, it might be safe to retire to my room, made my way thither.

As I started to get into something loose, I continued to brood on what he had told me about Aunt Dahlia. I found myself mystified. At dinner I had, of course, been distrait and preoccupied, but even so I would, I thought, have noticed if she had shown any signs of being in the grip of a wasting sickness or anything of that kind. As far as I could recollect, she had appeared to be tucking into the various items on the menu with her customary zip and *brio*. Yet Uncle Tom had spoken of her as looking as pale as a ghost, a thing which took some doing with a face as red as hers.

Odd, not to say mysterious.

I was still musing on this and wondering what Osborne Cross, the sleuth in *The Mystery of the Pink Crayfish*, would have made of it, when I was jerked out of my meditations by the turning of the door handle. This was followed by a forceful bang on the panel, and I realized how prudent I had been in locking up before settling in for the night. For the voice that now spoke was that of Stilton Cheesewright.

"Wooster!"

I rose, laying down my *Crayfish,* into which I had been about to dip, and put my lips to the keyhole.

"Wooster!"

"All right, my good fellow," I said coldly. "I heard you the first time. What do you want?"

"A word with you."

"Well, you jolly well aren't going to have it. Leave me, Cheesewright. I would be alone. I have a slight headache."

"It won't be slight, if I get at you."

"Ah, but you can't get at me," I riposted cleverly, and returning to my chair resumed my literary studies, pleasantly conscious of having worsted him in debate. He called me a few derogatory names through the woodwork, banged and handle-rattled a bit more, and finally shoved off, no doubt muttering horrid imprecations.

It was about five minutes later that there was another knock on the door, this time so soft and discreet that I had no difficulty in identifying it.

"Is that you, Jeeves?"

"Yes, sir."

"Just a moment."

As I crossed the room to admit him, I was surprised to find that the lower limbs were feeling a bit filleted. That verbal duel with my recent guest had shaken me more than I had suspected.

"I have just had a visit from Stilton Cheesewright, Jeeves," I said.

"Indeed, sir? I trust the outcome was satisfactory."

"Yes, I rather nonplused the simple soul. He had imagined that he could penetrate into my sanctum without let or hindrance, and was struck all of a heap when he found the door locked. But the episode has left me a little weak, and I would be glad if you could dig me out a whisky-and-soda."

"Certainly, sir."

"It wants to be prepared in just the right way. Who was that pal of yours you were speaking about the other day whose strength was as the strength of ten?"

"A gentleman of the name of Galahad, sir. You err, however, in supposing him to have been a personal friend. He was the subject of a poem by the late Alfred, Lord Tennyson."

"Immaterial, Jeeves. All I was going to say was that I would like the strength of this whisky-and-soda to be as that of ten. Don't flinch when pouring."

"Very good, sir."

He departed on his errand of mercy, and I buckled down to the *Crayfish* once more. But scarcely had I started to collect clues and interview suspects when I was interrupted again. A clenched fist had sloshed against the portal with a disturbing booming sound. Assuming that my visitor was Stilton, I was about to rise and rebuke him through the keyhole as before, when there penetrated from the outer spaces an ejaculation so fruity and full of vigor that it could have proceeded only from the lips of one who had learned her stuff among the hounds and foxes.

"Aunt Dahlia?"

"Open this door!"

I did so, and she came charging in.

"Where's Jeeves?" she asked, so plainly all of a twitter that I eyed her in considerable alarm. After what Uncle Tom had been saying about her tottering I didn't like this febrile agitation.

"Is something the matter?" I asked.

"You bet something's the matter, Bertie," said the old relative, sinking on to the chaise longue and looking as if at any moment she might start blowing bubbles, "I'm up against it, and only Jeeves can save my name in the home from becoming mud. Produce the blighter, and let him exercise that brain of his as never before."

12

I ENDEAVORED TO SOOTHE HER with a kindly pat on the top-knot.

"Jeeves will be back in a moment," I said, "and will doubtless put everything right with one wave of his magic wand. Tell me, my fluttering old aspen, what seems to be the trouble?"

She gulped like a stricken bull pup. I had rarely seen a more jittery aunt.

"It's Tom!"

"The uncle of that name?"

"How many Toms do you think there are in this joint, for goodness' sake?" she said, with a return of her normal forcefulness. "Yes, Thomas Portarlington Travers, my husband."

"Portarlington?" I said, a little shocked.

"He came pottering into my room just now."

I nodded intelligently. I remembered that he had spoken of having done so. It was on that occasion, you recall, that he had observed her pressing her hand to the top of her head.

"I see. Yes, so far I follow you. Scene, your room. Discovered sitting, you. Enter Uncle Tom, pottering. What then?"

116

She was silent for a space. Then she spoke in what was for her a hushed voice. That is to say, while rattling the vases on the mantelpiece, it did not bring plaster down from the ceiling.

"I'd better tell you the whole thing."

"Do, old ancestor. Nothing like getting it off the chest, whatever it is."

She gulped like another stricken bull pup.

"It's not a long story."

"Good," I said, for the hour was late and I had had a busy day.

"You remember when we were talking after you got here this evening . . . Bertie, you revolting object," she said, deviating momentarily from the main thread, "that moustache of yours is the most obscene thing I ever saw outside a nightmare. It seems to take one straight into another and a dreadful world. What made you commit this rash act?"

I tut-tutted a bit austerely.

"Never mind my moustache, old flesh and blood. You leave it alone, and it'll leave you alone. When we were talking this evening, you were saying?"

She accepted the rebuke with a moody nod.

"Yes, I mustn't get side-tracked. I must stick to the point."

"Like glue."

"When we were talking this evening, you said you wondered how I had managed to get Tom to cough up the price of that Daphne Dolores Morehead serial. You remember?"

"I do. I'm still wondering."

"Well, it's quite simple. I didn't."

"Eh?"

"Tom didn't contribute a penny."

"Then how—?"

"I'll tell you how. I pawned my pearl necklace."

I gazed at her . . . well, I suppose "awestruck" would be the word. Acquaintance with this woman dating from the days when I was an infant mewling and puking in my nurse's arms, if you will excuse the expression, had left me with the feeling that her guiding motto in life was "Anything goes," but this seemed pretty advanced stuff even for one to whom the sky had always been the limit.

"Pawned it?" I said.

"Pawned it."

"Hocked it, you mean? Popped it? Put it up the spout?"

"That's right. It was the only thing to do. I had to have that serial in order to salt the mine, and Tom absolutely refused to give me so much as a fiver to slake the thirst for gold of this blood-sucking Morehead. 'Nonsense, nonsense,' he kept saying. 'Quite out of the question, quite out of the question.' So I slipped up to London, took the necklace to Aspinall's, told them to make a replica, and then went along to the pawnbroker's. Well, when I say pawnbroker's, that's a figure of speech. My fellow was much higher class. More of a moneylender, you would call him."

I whistled a bar or two.

"Then that thing I picked up for you this morning was a dud?"

"Cultured stuff."

"Golly!" I said. "You aunts do live!" I hesitated. I was loath to bruise that gentle spirit, especially at a moment when she was worried about something, but it seemed to me a nephew's duty to point out the snag. "And when . . . I'm afraid this is going to spoil your day, but what happens when Uncle Tom finds out?"

"That's exactly the trouble."

"I thought it might be."

She gulped like a third stricken bull pup.

"If it hadn't been for a foul bit of bad luck, he wouldn't have found out in a million years. I don't suppose Tom, bless him, would know the difference between the Kohinoor and something from Woolworth's."

I saw her point. Uncle Tom, as I have indicated, is a red-hot collector of old silver and there is nothing you can teach him about sconces, foliation, scrolls, and ribbon wreaths, but jewelry is to him, as to most of the male sex, a sealed book.

"But he's going to find out tomorrow evening, and I'll tell you why. I told you he came to my room just now. Well, we had been kidding back and forth for a few moments, all very pleasant and matey, when he suddenly . . . Oh, my God!"

I administered another sympathetic pat on the bean.

"Pull yourself together, old relative. What did he suddenly do?"

"He suddenly told me that this Lord Sidcup who is coming tomorrow is not only an old-silver hound but an expert on jewelry, and he was going to ask him, while here, to take a look at my necklace."

"Gosh!"

"He said he had often had a suspicion that the bandits who sold it to him had taken advantage of his innocence and charged him a lot too much. Sidcup, he said, would be able to put him straight about it."

"Golly!"

" 'Gosh!' is right, and so is 'Golly!' "

"Then that's why you clutched the top of your head and tottered?"

"That's why. How long do you suppose it will take this fiend in human shape to see through that dud string of pearls and spill the beans? Just about ten seconds, if not less. And then what? Can you blame me for tottering?"

I certainly couldn't. In her place, I would have tottered myself and tottered like nobody's business. A far duller man than Bertram Wooster would have been able to appreciate that this aunt who sat before me clutching feverishly at her perm was an aunt who was in the dickens of a spot. A crisis had been precipitated in her affairs which threatened, unless some pretty adroit staffwork was pulled by her friends and well-wishers, to put the home right plumb spang in the melting pot.

I have made a rather close study of the married state, and I know what happens when one turtle dove gets the goods on the other turtle dove. Bingo Little has often told me that if Mrs. Bingo had managed to get on him some of the things it seemed likely she was going to get, the moon would have been turned to blood and Civilization shaken to its foundations. I have heard much the same thing from other husbands of my acquaintance, and of course similar upheavals occur when it is the little woman who is caught bending.

Always up to now Aunt Dahlia had been the boss of Brinkley Court, maintaining a strong centralized government, but let Uncle Tom discover that she had pawned her pearl necklace in order to buy a serial story for what for some reason he always alluded to as *Madame's Nightshirt,* a periodical which from the very start he had never liked, and she would be in much the same position as one of those monarchs or dictators who wake up one morning to find that the populace had risen against them and is saying it with bombs. Uncle Tom is a kindly old bimbo, but even kindly old bimbos can make themselves dashed unpleasant when the conditions are right.

"Egad!" I said, fingering the chin. "This is not so good."

"It's the end of all things."

"You say this Sidcup bird will be here tomorrow? It doesn't give you much time to put your affairs in order. No wonder you're sending out S.O.S.'s for Jeeves."

"Only he can save me from the fate that is worse than death."

"But can even Jeeves adjust matters?"

"I'm banking on him. After all, he's a hell of an adjuster."

"True."

"He's got you out of some deepish holes in his time."

"Quite. I often say there is none like him, none. He should be with us at any moment now. He stepped out to get me a tankard of the old familiar juice."

Her eyes gleamed with a strange light.

"Bags I first go at it!"

I patted her hand.

"Of course," I said, "of course. You may take that as read. You don't find Bertram Wooster hogging the drink supply when a suffering aunt is at his side with her tongue hanging out. Your need is greater than mine, as whoever-it-was said to the stretcher case. Ah!"

Jeeves had come in bearing the elixir, not a split second before we were ready for it. I took the beaker from him and offered it to the aged relative with a courteous gesture. With a brief "Mud in your eye" she drank deeply. I then finished what was left at a gulp.

"Oh, Jeeves," I said.

"Sir?"

"Lend me your ears."

"Very good, sir."

It had needed but a glance at my late father's sister to tell me that if there was going to be any lucid exposition of the *res,* I was the one who would have to attend to it. After moistening her clay she had relapsed into a sort of frozen coma, staring before her with unseeing eyes and showing a disposition to pant like a hart when heated in the chase. Nor was this to be wondered at. Few women would have been in vivacious mood, had Fate touched off beneath them a similar stick of trinitrotoluol. I imagine her emotions after Uncle Tom had said his say must have been of much the same nature as those which she had no doubt frequently experienced in her hunting days when her steed, having bucked her from the saddle, had proceeded to roll on her. And while the blushful Hippocrene of which she had just imbibed her share had been robust and full of inner meaning, it had obviously merely scratched the surface.

"A rather tight place has popped up out of a trap, Jeeves, and we should be glad of your counsel and advice. This is the posish. Aunt Dahlia has a pearl necklace, the Christmas gift of Uncle Tom, whose second name, I'll bet you didn't know, is Portarlington. The one you picked up at Aspinall's this morning. Are you with me?"

"Yes, sir."

"Well, this is where the plot thickens. It isn't a pearl necklace, if I make my meaning clear. For reasons into which we need not go, she put the Uncle-Tom-Merry-Christmas one up the spout. What is now in her possession is an imitation of little or no intrinsic value."

"Yes, sir."

"You don't seem amazed."

"No, sir. I became aware of the fact when I saw the

necklace this morning. I perceived at once that what had been given to me was a cultured replica."

"Good Lord! Was it as easy to spot as that?"

"Oh, no, sir. I have no doubt that it would deceive the untutored eye. But I spent some months at one time studying jewelry under the auspices of a cousin of mine who is in the trade. The genuine pearl has no core."

"No what?"

"Core, sir. In its interior. The cultured pearl has. A cultured pearl differs from a real one in this respect, that it is the result of introducing into the oyster a foreign substance designed to irritate it and induce it to coat the substance with layer upon layer of nacre. Nature's own irritant is invariably so small as to be invisible, but the core in the cultured imitation can be discerned, as a rule merely by holding the cultured pearl up before a strong light. This was what I did in the matter of Mrs. Travers's necklace. I had no need of the endoscope."

"The what?"

"Endoscope, sir. An instrument which enables one to peer into the cultured pearl's interior and discern the core."

I was conscious of a passing pang for the oyster world, feeling—and I think correctly—that life for these unfortunate bivalves must be one damn thing after another, but my principal emotion was one of astonishment.

"Great Scott, Jeeves! Do you know everything?"

"Oh, no, sir. It just happens that jewelry is something of a hobby of mine. With diamonds, of course, the test would be different. One might ascertain the genuineness of a diamond, for example, by taking a sapphire-point phonograph needle—which is, as you are no doubt aware, corundum having a hardness of 9—and trying to make a small test scratch on the underside of the suspect stone. A genuine diamond, I need scarcely remind you, is the only substance with a hardness of 10—Moh's scale of hardness. Most of the hard objects we see about us are approximately 7 in the hardness scale. But you were saying, sir?"

I was still blinking a bit. When Jeeves gets going nicely, he often has this effect on me. With a strong effort I pulled myself together and was able to continue.

"Well, that's the nub of the story," I said. "Aunt Dahlia's necklace, the one now in her possession, is, as your trained senses told you, a seething mass of cores and not worth the paper it's written on. Right. Well, here's the point. If no complications had been introduced into the scenario, all would be well, because Uncle Tom couldn't tell the difference between a real necklace and an imitation one if he tried for months. But a whale of a complication has been introduced. A pal of his is coming tomorrow to look at the thing, and this pal, like you, is an expert on jewelry. You see what will happen the moment he cocks an eye at the worthless substitute. Exposure, ruin, desolation, and despair. Uncle Tom, learning the truth, will blow his top, and Aunt Dahlia's prestige will be down among the wines and spirits. You get me, Jeeves?"

"Yes, sir."

"Then let us have your views."

"It is disturbing, sir."

I wouldn't have thought that anything would have been able to rouse that crushed aunt from her trance, but this did the trick. She came up like a rocketing pheasant from the chair into which she had slumped.

"Disturbing! What a word to use!"

I sympathized with her distress, but checked her with an upraised hand.

"Please, old relative! Yes, Jeeves, it is, as you say, a bit on the disturbing side, but one feels that you will probably have something constructive to place before the board. We shall be glad to hear your solution."

He allowed a muscle at the side of his mouth to twitch regretfully.

"With a problem of such magnitude, sir, I fear I am not able to provide a solution offhand, if I may use the expression. I should require to give the matter thought. Perhaps if I might be permitted to pace the corridor for awhile?"

"Certainly, Jeeves. Pace all the corridors you wish."

"Thank you, sir. I shall hope to return shortly with some suggestion which will give satisfaction."

I closed the door behind him and turned to the aged r., who, her face bright purple, was still muttering "Disturbing."

"I know just how you feel, old flesh and blood," I said. "I ought to have warned you that Jeeves never leaps about and rolls the eyes when you spring something sensational on him, preferring to preserve the calm impassivity of a stuffed frog."

"Disturbing!"

"I have grown not to mind this much myself, though occasionally, as I was about to do tonight, administering a rather stern rebuke, for experience has taught me—"

"Disturbing, for God's sake! *Disturbing!*"

"I know, I know. That manner of his does afflict the nerve centers quite a bit, does it not? But, as I was saying, experience has taught me that there always follows some ripe solution of whatever the problem may be. As the fellow said, if stuffed frogs come, can ripe solutions be far behind?"

She sat up. I could see the light of hope dawning in her eyes.

"You really think he will find the way?"

"I am convinced of it. He always finds the way. I wish I had a quid for every way he has found since first he started to serve under the Wooster banner. Remember how he enabled me to put it across Roderick Spode at Totleigh Towers."

"He did, didn't he?"

"He certainly did. One moment, Spode was a dark menace, the next a mere blob of jelly with all his fangs removed, groveling at my feet. You can rely implicitly on Jeeves. Ah," I said, as the door opened. "Here he comes, his head sticking out at the back and his eyes shining with intelligence and what not. You have thought of something, Jeeves?"

"Yes, sir."

"I knew it. I was saying a moment ago that you always find the way. Well, let us have it."

"There is a method by means of which Mrs. Travers can be extricated from her sea of troubles. Shakespeare."

I didn't know why he was addressing me as Shakespeare, but I motioned him to continue.

"Proceed, Jeeves."

He did so, turning now to Aunt Dahlia, who was gazing at him like a bear about to receive a bun.

"If, as Mr. Wooster has told me, madam, this jewelry expert is to be with us shortly, it would seem that your best plan is to cause the necklace to disappear before he arrives. If I may make my meaning clearer, madam," he went on in response to a query from the sizzling woman as to whether he supposed her to be a bally conjurer. "What I had in mind was something in the nature of a burglarious entry, as the result of which the piece of jewelry would be abstracted. You will readily see, madam, that if the gentleman, coming to examine the necklace, finds that there is no necklace for him to examine—"

"He won't be able to examine it?"

"Precisely, madam. *Rem acu tetigisti.*"

I shook the lemon. I had expected something better than this. It seemed to me that that great brain had at last come unglued, and this saddened me.

"But, Jeeves," I said gently, "where do you get your burglar? From the Army and Navy Stores?"

"I was thinking that you might consent to undertake the task, sir."

"Me?"

"Gosh, yes," said Aunt Dahlia, her dial lighting up like a stage moon. "How right you are, Jeeves. You wouldn't mind doing a little thing like that for me, would you, Bertie? Of course you wouldn't. You've grasped the idea? You get a ladder, prop it up against my window, pop in, pinch the necklace and streak off with it. And tomorrow I go to Tom in floods of tears and say 'Tom! My pearls! They've gone! Some low bounder sneaked in last night and snitched them as I slept.' That's the idea, isn't it, Jeeves?"

"Precisely, madam. It would be a simple task for Mr. Wooster. I notice that since my last visit to Brinkley Court the bars which protected the windows have been removed."

"Yes, I had that done after that time when we were all locked out. You remember?"

"Very vividly, madam."

"So there's nothing to stop you, Bertie."

"Nothing but—"

I paused. I had been about to say "Nothing but my total and absolute refusal to take on the assignment in any shape or form," but I checked the words before they could pass the lips. I saw that I was exaggerating what I had supposed to be the dangers and difficulties of the enterprise.

After all, I felt, there was nothing so very hazardous about it. All I had to do was to procure a ladder and climb up it, a ludicrously simple feat for one of my agility and lissomness. A nuisance, of course, having to turn out at this time of night, but I was quite prepared to do so in order to bring the roses back to the cheeks of a woman who in my bib and cradle days had frequently dandled me on her knee, not to mention saving my life on one occasion when I had half swallowed a rubber comforter.

"Nothing at all," I replied cordially. "Nothing whatever. You provide the necklace, and I will do the rest. Which is your room?"

"The last one on the left."

"Right."

"Left, fool. I'll be going there now, so as to be in readiness. Golly, Jeeves, you've taken a weight off my mind. I feel a new woman. You won't mind if you hear me singing about the house?"

"Not at all, madam."

"I shall probably start first thing tomorrow."

"Any time that suits you, madam."

He closed the door behind her with an indulgent smile, or something as nearly resembling a smile as he ever allows to appear on his map.

"One is glad to see Mrs. Travers so happy, sir."

"Yes, you certainly bucked her up like a tonic. No difficulty about finding a ladder, I take it?"

"Oh, no, sir. I chanced to observe one outside the tool shed by the kitchen garden."

"So did I, now you mention it. No doubt it's still there, so let's go. If it were . . . what's that expression of yours?"

"If it were done when 'tis done, then 'twere well it were done quickly, sir."

"That's right. No sense in standing humming and haw-ing."

"No, sir. There is a tide in the affairs of men which, taken at the flood, leads on to fortune."

"Exactly," I said.

I couldn't have put it better myself.

The venture went with gratifying smoothness. I found the ladder, by the tool shed as foreshadowed, and lugged it across country to the desired spot. I propped it up. I climbed it. In next to no time I was through the window and moving silently across the floor.

Well, not so dashed silently, as a matter of fact, because I collided with a table which happened to be in the fair-way and upset it with quite a bit of noise.

"Who's there?" asked a voice from the darkness in a startled sort of way.

This tickled me. Ah, I said to myself amusedly, Aunt Dahlia throwing herself into her part and giving the thing just the touch it needed to make it box-office. What an artist, I felt.

Then it said "Who's there?" again, and it was as though a well-iced hand had been laid upon my heart.

Because the voice was not the voice of any ruddy aunt, it was the voice of Florence Craye. The next moment light flooded the apartment and there she was, sitting up in bed in a pink boudoir cap.

13

I DON'T KNOW if you happen to be familiar with a poem called "The Charge of the Light Brigade" by the bird Tennyson whom Jeeves had mentioned when speaking of the fellow whose strength was as the strength of ten. It is, I believe, fairly well known, and I used to have to recite it at the age of seven or thereabouts when summoned to the drawing-room to give visitors a glimpse of the young Wooster. "Bertie recites so nicely," my mother used to say—getting her facts twisted, I may mention, because I practically always fluffed my lines—and after trying to duck for safety and being hauled back I would snap into it. And very unpleasant the whole thing was, so people have told me.

Well, what I was about to say, when I rambled off a bit on the subject of the dear old days, was that though in the course of the years most of the poem of which I speak has slid from the memory, I still recall its punch line. The thing goes, as you probably know,

> *Tum tiddle umpty-pum*
> *Tum tiddle umpty-pum*
> *Tum tiddle umpty-pum*

and this brought you to the snapperoo or payoff, which was

Someone had blundered

I always remember that bit, and the reason I bring it up now is that, as I stood blinking at this pink-boudoir-capped girl, I was feeling just as those Light Brigade fellows must have felt. Obviously someone had blundered here, and that someone was Aunt Dahlia. Why she should have told me that her window was the last one on the left, when the last one on the left was what it was anything but, was more than I could imagine. One sought in vain for what Stilton Cheesewright would have called the ulterior motive.

However, it is hopeless to try to fathom the mental processes of aunts, and anyway this was no time for idle speculation. The first thing the man of sensibility has to do on arriving like a sack of coals in a girl's bedroom in the small hours is to get the conversation going, and it was to this that I now addressed myself. Nothing is worse on these occasions than the awkward pause and the embarrassed silence.

"Oh, hullo," I said, as brightly and cheerily as I could manage. "I say, I'm most frightfully sorry to pop in like this at a moment when you were doubtless knitting up the ravelled sleave of care, but I went for a breather in the garden and found I was locked out, so I thought my best plan was not to rouse the house but to nip in through the first open window. You know how it is when you rouse houses. They don't like it."

I would have spoken further, developing the theme, for it seemed to me that I was on the right lines . . . so much better, I mean to say, than affecting to be walking in my sleep. All that *Where am I?* stuff, I mean. Too damn silly . . . but she suddenly gave one of those rippling laughs of hers.

"Oh, Bertie!" she said, and not, mark you, with that sort of weary fed-up-ness with which girls generally say "Oh, Bertie!" to me. "What a romantic you are!"

"Eh?"

She rippled again. It was a relief, of course, to find that she did not propose to yell for help and all that sort of thing, but I must say I found this mirth a bit difficult to cope with. You've probably had the same experience yourself—listening to people guffawing like hyenas and not having the foggiest what the joke is. It makes you feel at a disadvantage.

She was looking at me in an odd kind of way, as if at some child for whom, while conceding that it had water on the brain, she felt a fondness.

"Isn't this just the sort of thing you would do!" she said. "I told you I was no longer engaged to D'Arcy Cheese-wright, and you had to fly to me. You couldn't wait till the morning, could you? I suppose you had some sort of idea of kissing me softly while I slept?"

I leaped perhaps six inches in the direction of the ceiling. I was appalled, and I think not unjustifiably so. I mean, dash it, a fellow who has always prided himself on the scrupulous delicacy of his relations with the other sex doesn't like to have it supposed that he deliberately shins up ladders at one in the morning in order to kiss girls while they sleep.

"Good Lord, no," I said, replacing the chair which I had knocked over in my agitation. "Nothing further from my thoughts. I take it your attention happened to wander for a moment when I was outlining the facts just now. What I was saying, only you weren't listening, was that I went for a breather in the garden and found I was locked out—"

She rippled once more. That looking-fondly-at-idiot-child expression on her face had become intensified.

"You don't think I'm angry, do you? Of course I'm not. I'm very touched. Kiss me, Bertie."

Well, one has to be civil. I did as directed, but with an uneasy feeling that this was a bit above the odds. I didn't at all like the general trend of affairs, the whole thing seeming to me to be becoming far too French. When I broke out of the clinch and stepped back, I found the expression on her face had changed. She was now regarding me in a sort of speculative way, if you know what I mean, rather like a governess taking a gander at the new pupil.

"Mother's quite wrong," she said.

"Mother?"

"Your Aunt Agatha."

This surprised me.

"You call her Mother? Oh, well, okay, if you like it. Up to you, of course. What was she wrong about?"

"You. She keeps insisting that you are a vapid and irreflective nitwit who ought years ago to have been put in some good mental home."

I drew myself up haughtily, cut more or less to the quick. So this was how the woman was accustomed to shoot off her bally head about me in my absence, was it! A pretty state of affairs. The woman, I'll trouble you, whose repulsive son Thos I had for years practically nursed in my bosom. That is to say, when he passed through London on his way back to school, I put him up at my residence and not only fed him luxuriously but with no thought of self took him to the Old Vic and Madame Tussaud's. Was there no gratitude in the world?

"She does, does she?"

"She's awfully amusing about you."

"Amusing, eh?"

"It was she who said that you had a brain like a peahen."

Here, of course, if I had wished to take it, was an admirable opportunity to go into this matter of peahens and ascertain just where they stood in the roster of our feathered friends as regarded the I.Q., but I let it go.

She adjusted the boudoir cap, which the recent embrace had tilted a bit to one side. She was still looking at me in that speculative way.

"She says you are a guffin."

"A what?"

"A guffin."

"I don't understand you."

"It's one of those old-fashioned expressions. What she meant, I think, was that she considered you a wet smack and a total loss. But I told her she was quite mistaken and that there is a lot more in you than people suspect. I realized that when I found you in that bookshop that day buying *Spindrift*. Do you remember?"

I had not forgotten the incident. The whole thing had been one of those unfortunate misunderstandings. I had promised Jeeves to buy him the works of a cove of the name of Spinoza—some kind of philosopher or something, I gathered—and the chap at the bookshop, expressing the opinion that there was no such person as Spinoza, had handed me *Spindrift* as being more probably what I was after, and scarcely had I grasped it when Florence came in. To assume that I had purchased the thing and to autograph it for me in green ink with her fountain pen had been with her the work of an instant.

"I knew then that you were groping dimly for the light and trying to educate yourself by reading good literature, that there was something lying hidden deep down in you that only needed bringing out. It would be a fascinating task, I told myself, fostering the latent potentialities of your budding mind. Like watching over some timid, backward flower."

I bridled pretty considerably. Timid, backward flower, my left eyeball, I was thinking. I was on the point of saying something stinging like "Oh, yes?" when she proceeded.

"I know I can mold you, Bertie. You want to improve yourself, and that is half the battle. What have you been reading lately?"

"Well, what with one thing and another, my reading has been a bit cut into these last days, but I am in the process of plugging away at a thing called *The Mystery of the Pink Crayfish.*"

Her slender frame was more or less hidden beneath the bedclothes, but I got the impression that a shudder had run through it.

"Oh, Bertie!" she said, this time with something more nearly approaching the normal intonation.

"Well, it's dashed good," I insisted stoutly. "This baronet, this Sir Eustace Willoughby, is discovered in his library with his head bashed in—"

A look of pain came into her face.

"Please!" She sighed. "Oh, dear," she said, "I'm afraid it's going to be uphill work fostering the latent potentialities of your budding mind."

"I wouldn't try, if I were you. Give it a miss, is my advice."

"But I hate to think of leaving you in the darkness, doing nothing but smoke and drink at the Drones Club."

I put her straight about this. She had her facts wrong.

"I also play Darts."

"Darts!"

"As a matter of fact, I shall very soon be this year's club champion. The event is a snip for me. Ask anybody."

"How can you fritter away your time like that, when you might be reading T. S. Eliot? I would like to see you—"

What it was she would have liked to see me doing she did not say, though I presumed it was something foul and educational, for at this juncture someone knocked on the door.

It was the last contingency I had been anticipating, and it caused my heart to leap like a salmon in the spawning season and become entangled with my front teeth. I looked at the door with what I have heard Jeeves call a wild surmise, and persp. breaking out on my brow.

Florence, I noticed, seemed a bit startled, too. One gathered that she hadn't expected, when setting out for Brinkley Court, that her bedroom was going to be such a social center. There's a song I used to sing a good deal at one time, the refrain or burthen of which began with the words "Let's all go round to Maud's." Much the same sentiment appeared to be animating the guests beneath Aunt Dahlia's roof, and it was, of course, upsetting for the poor child. At one in the morning girls like a bit of privacy, and she couldn't have had much less privacy if she had been running a snack bar on a racecourse.

"Who's that?" she cried.

"Me," responded a deep, resonant voice, and Florence clapped a hand to her throat, a thing I didn't know anybody ever did off the stage.

For the d.r.v. was that of G. D'Arcy Cheesewright. To cut a long story short, the man was in again.

It was with a distinctly fevered hand that Florence reached out for a dressing gown, and in her deportment, as she hopped from between the sheets, I noted a marked suggestion of a pea on a hot shovel. She is one of those cool, calm, well-poised modern girls from whom as a rule you can seldom get more than a raised eyebrow, but I could see that this thing of having Stilton a pleasant visitor at a moment when her room was all cluttered up with Woosters had rattled her more than slightly.

"What do you want?"

"I have brought your letters."

"Leave them on the mat."

"I will not leave them on the mat. I wish to confront you in person."

"At this time of night! You aren't coming in here!"

"That," said Stilton crisply, "is where you make your ruddy error. I *am* coming in there."

I remember Jeeves saying something once about the poet's eye in a fine frenzy rolling and glancing from Heaven to earth, from earth to Heaven. It was in much the same manner that Florence's eye now rolled and glanced. I could see what was disturbing her, of course. It was that old problem which always bothers chaps in mystery thrillers—viz. how to get rid of the body—in this case, that of Bertram. If Stilton proposed to enter, it was essential that Bertram be placed in storage somewhere for the time being, but the question that arose was where.

There was a cupboard on the other side of the room, and she nipped across and flung open the door.

"Quick!" she hissed, and it's all rot to say you can't hiss a word that hasn't an 's' in it. She did it on her head. "In here!"

The suggestion struck me as a good one. I popped in and she closed the door behind me.

Well, actually, the fingers being, I suppose, nerveless, she didn't, but left it ajar. I was able, consequently, to follow the ensuing conversation as clearly as if it had been coming over the wireless.

Stilton began it.

"Here are your letters," he said stiffly.

"Thank you," she said stiffly.

"Don't mention it," he said stiffly.

"Put them on the dressing table," she said stiffly.

"Right ho," he said stiffly.

I don't know when I've known a bigger night for stiff speakers.

After a brief interval, during which I presumed that he was depositing the correspondence as directed, Stilton resumed.

"You got my telegram?"

"Of course I got your telegram."

"You notice I have shaved my moustache?"

"I do."

"What do you mean, my underhanded skulduggery?"

"It was my first move on finding out about your underhanded skulduggery."

"If you don't call it underhanded skulduggery, sneaking off to night clubs with the louse Wooster, it would be extremely entertaining to be informed how you would describe it."

"You know perfectly well that I wanted atmosphere for my book."

"Ho!"

"And don't say 'Ho.'"

"I will say 'Ho!' " retorted Stilton with spirit. "Your book, my foot. I don't believe there is any book. I don't believe you've ever written a book."

"Indeed? How about *Spindrift*, now in its fifth edition and soon to be translated into the Scandinavian?"

"Probably the work of the louse Gorringe."

I imagine that at this coarse insult Florence's eyes flashed fire. The voice in which she spoke certainly suggested it.

"Mr. Cheesewright, you have had a couple!"

"Nothing of the kind."

"Then you must be insane, and I wish you would have the courtesy to take that pumpkin head of yours out of here."

I rather think, though I can't be sure, that at these words Stilton ground his teeth. Certainly there was a peculiar sound, as if a coffee mill had sprung into action. The voice that filtered through to my cozy retreat quivered hoarsely.

"My head is not like a pumpkin!"

"It is, too, like a pumpkin."

"It is not like a pumpkin at all. I have this on the authority of Bertie Wooster, who says it is more like the dome of St. Paul's." He broke off, and there was a smacking sound. He had apparently smitten his brow. "Wooster!" he cried, emitting an animal snarl. "I didn't come here to talk about my head, I came to talk about Wooster, the slithery serpent who slinks behind chaps' backs, stealing fellows' girls from them. Wooster the home-wrecker! Wooster the snake in the grass from whom no woman is safe! Wooster the modern Don what's-his-name! You've been conducting a clandestine intrigue with him right along. You thought you were fooling me, didn't you? You thought I didn't see through your pitiful . . . your pitiful . . . Dammit, what's the word? . . . your pitiful . . . No, it's gone."

"I wish you would follow its excellent example."

"Subterfuges! I knew I'd get it. Do you think I didn't see through your pitiful subterfuges? All that bilge about wanting me to grow a moustache. Do you think I'm not on to it that the whole of that moustache sequence was just a ruse to enable you to break it off with me and switch over to the grass snake Wooster? 'How can I get rid of this Cheesewright?' you said to yourself. 'Ha, I have it!' you said to yourself. 'I'll tell him he's got to grow a moustache. He'll say like hell he'll grow any bally moustache. And then I'll say Ho! You won't won't you? All right, then all is over between us. That'll fix it.' It must have been a nasty shock to you when I yielded to your request. Upset your plans quite a bit, I imagine? You hadn't bargained for that, had you?"

Florence spoke in a voice that would have frozen an Eskimo.

"The door is just behind you, Mr. Cheesewright. It opens if you turn the handle."

He came right back at her.

"Never mind the door. I'm talking about you and the leper Wooster. I suppose you will now hitch on to him, or what's left of him after I've finished stepping on his face. Am I right?"

"You are."

"It is your intention to marry this human gumboil?"

"It is."

"Ho!"

Well, I don't know how you would have behaved in my place, hearing these words and realizing for the first time that the evil had spread as far as this. You would probably have started violently, as I did. No doubt I ought to have spotted the impending doom, but for some reason or other, possibly because I had been devoting so much thought to Stilton, I hadn't. This abrupt announcement of my betrothal to a girl of whom I took the gravest view shook me to my depths, with the result, as I say, that I started violently.

And, of course, the one place where it is unwise to start violently, if you wish to remain unobserved and incognito, is a cupboard in a female bedroom. What exactly it was that now rained down on me, dislodged by my sudden movement, I cannot say, but I think it was hat boxes. Whatever it was, it sounded in the stilly night like coal being lowered down a chute into a cellar, and I heard a sharp exclamation. A moment later a hand wrenched open the door and a suffused face glared in on me as I brushed the hat boxes, if they were hat boxes, from my hair.

"Ho!" said Stilton, speaking with difficulty like a cat with a fishbone in its throat. "Come on out of there, serpent," he added, attaching himself to my left ear and pulling vigorously.

I emerged like a cork out of a bottle.

14

IT IS ALWAYS a bit difficult to know just what to say on occasions like this. I said "Oh, there you are, Stilton. Nice evening," but it seemed to be the wrong thing, for he merely quivered as if he had got a beetle down his back and increased the incandescence of his gaze. I saw that it was going to require quite a good deal of suavity and tact on my part to put us all at our ease.

"You are doubtless surprised—" I began, but he held up a hand as if he had been back in the Force directing the traffic. He then spoke in a quiet, if rumbling, voice.

"You will find me waiting in the corridor, Wooster," he said, and strode out.

I understood the spirit which had prompted the words. It was the *preux chevalier* in him coming to the surface. You can stir up a Cheesewright till he froths at the mouth, but you cannot make him forget that he is an Old Etonian and a pukka Sahib. Old Etonians do not brawl in the presence of the other sex. Nor do pukka Sahibs. They wait till they are alone with the party of the second part in some secluded nook.

I thoroughly approved of this fineness of feeling, for it had left me sitting on top of the world. It would now, I saw, be possible for me to avoid anything in the nature of unpleasantness by executing one of those subtle rearward movements which great Generals keep up their sleeves for moments when things are beginning to get too hot. You think you have got one of these Generals cornered and are all ready to swoop on him, and it is with surprise and chagrin that, just as you are pulling up your socks and putting a final polish on your weapons, you observe that he isn't there. He has withdrawn on his strategic railway, taking his troops with him.

With that ladder waiting in readiness for me, I was in a similarly agreeable position. Corridors meant nothing to me. I didn't need to go into any corridors. All I had to do was slide through the window, place my foot on the top rung and carry on with a light heart to terra firma.

But there is one circumstance which can dish the greatest of Generals—viz. if, toddling along to the station to buy his ticket, he finds that since he last saw it the strategic railway has been blown up. That is the time when you will find him scratching his head and chewing the lower lip. And it was a disaster of this nature that now dished me. Approaching the window and glancing out, I saw that the ladder was no longer there. At some point in the course of the recent conversations it had vanished, leaving not a wrack behind.

What had become of it was a mystery I found myself unable to solve, but that was a thing that could be gone into later. At the moment it was plain that the cream of the Wooster brain must be given to a more urgent matter—to wit, the question of how I was to get out of the room without passing through the door and finding myself alone in a confined space with Stilton, the last person in his present frame of mind with whom a man of slender physique would wish to be alone in confined spaces. I put this to Florence, and she agreed, like Sherlock Holmes, that the problem was one which undoubtedly presented certain points of interest.

"You can't stay here all night," she said.

I admitted the justice of this, but added that I didn't at the moment see what the dickens else I could do.

"You wouldn't care to knot your sheets and lower me to the ground with them?"

"No, I wouldn't. Why don't you jump?"

"And smash myself to hash?"

"You might not."

"On the other hand, I might."

"Well, you can't make an omelette without breaking eggs."

I gave her a look. It seemed to me the silliest thing I had ever heard a girl say, and I have heard girls say some pretty silly things in my time. I was on the point of saying "You and your bally omelettes!" when something seemed to go off with a pop in my brain and it was as though I had swallowed a brimming dose of some invigorating tonic, the sort of pick-me-up that makes a bedridden invalid rise from his couch and dance the Carioca. Bertram was himself again. With a steady hand I opened the door. And when Stilton advanced on me like a mass murderer about to do his stuff, I quelled him with the power of the human eye.

"Just a moment, Stilton," I said suavely. "Before you give rein, if that's the expression I want, to your angry passions, don't forget you've drawn me in the Drones Club Darts sweep."

It was enough. Halting abruptly, as if he had walked into a lamp post, he stood goggling like a cat in an adage. Cats in adages, Jeeves tells me, let "I dare not" wait upon

"I would," and I could see with the naked eye that this was what Stilton was doing.

Flicking a speck of dust from my sleeve and smiling a quiet smile, I proceeded to rub it in.

"You appreciate the position of affairs?" I said. "By drawing my name, you have set yourself apart from ordinary men. To make it clear to the meanest intelligence . . . I allude to yours, my dear Cheesewright . . . where the ordinary man, seeing me strolling along Piccadilly, merely says 'Ah, there goes Bertie Wooster,' you, having drawn me in the sweep, say 'There goes my fifty-six pounds ten shillings,' and you probably run after me to tell me to be very careful when crossing the street because the traffic nowadays is so dangerous."

He raised a hand and fingered his chin. I could see that my words were not being wasted. Shooting my cuffs, I resumed.

"In what sort of condition shall I be to win that Darts tourney and put nearly sixty quid in your pocket, if you pull the strong arm stuff you are contemplating? Try that one on your bazooka, my dear Cheesewright."

It was a tense struggle, of course, but it didn't last long. Reason prevailed. With a low grunt which spoke eloquently of the overwrought soul, he stepped back, and with a cheery "Well, good night, old man" and a benevolent wave of the hand I left him and made my way to my room.

As I entered it, Aunt Dahlia in a maroon dressing gown rose from the chair in which she had been sitting and fixed me with a blazing eye, struggling for utterance.

"Well!" she said, choking on the word like a Pekinese on a chump chop too large for its frail strength. After which, speech failing her, she merely stood and gargled.

I must say that this struck me in the circs as a bit thick.

I mean, if anyone was entitled to have blazing eyes and trouble with the vocal cords, it was, as I saw it, me. I mean, consider the facts. Owing to this woman's cloth-headed blundering when issuing divisional orders, I was slated to walk down the aisle with Florence Craye and had been subjected to an ordeal which might well have done permanent damage to the delicate nerve centers. I was strongly of the opinion that so far from being glared and gargled at I was in a position to demand a categorical explanation and to see that I got it.

As I cleared my throat in order to put this to her, she mastered her emotion sufficiently to be able to speak.

"Well?" she said, looking like a female minor prophet about to curse the sins of the people. "May I trespass on your valuable time long enough to ask you what in the name of everything bloodsome you think you're playing at, young piefaced Bertie? It is now some twenty minutes past one o'clock in the morning, and not a spot of action on your part. Do you expect me to sit up all night waiting for you to get around to a simple, easy task which a crippled child of six could have had all done and washed up in a quarter of an hour? I suppose this is just the shank of the evening to you dissipated Londoners, but we rustics like to get our sleep. What's the idea? Why the delay? What on earth have you been doing all this while, you revolting young piece of cheese?"

I laughed a hollow, mirthless laugh. Getting quite the wrong angle on it, she begged me to postpone my farm-yard imitations to a more suitable moment. I told myself that I must be calm . . . calm.

"Before replying to your questions, aged relative," I said, holding myself in with a strong effort, "let me put one to you. Would you mind informing me in a few simple

words why you told me that your window was the end one
on the left?"

"It is the end one on the left."

"Pardon me."

"Looking from the house."

"Oh, looking *from* the house?" A great light dawned on
me. "I thought you meant looking *at* the house."

"Looking at the house it would of course be . . . " She
broke off with a startled yowl, staring at me with quite a
good deal of that wild surmise stuff. "Don't tell me you got
into the wrong room?"

"It could scarcely have been wronger."

"Whose was it?"

"Florence Craye's."

She whistled. It was plain that the drama of the situation had not escaped her.

"Was she in bed?"

"With a pink boudoir cap on."

"And she woke up and found you there?"

"Almost immediately. I knocked over a table or something."

She whistled again.

"You'll have to marry the girl."

"Quite."

"Though I doubt if she would have you."

"I have positive inside information to the contrary."

"You fixed it up?"

"She fixed it up. We are affianced."

"In spite of that moustache?"

"She likes the moustache."

"She does? Morbid. But what about Cheesewright? I
thought he and she were affianced, as you call it?"

"No longer. It's off."

"They've bust up?"

"Completely."

"And now she's taken you on?"

"That's right."

A look of concern came into her face. Despite the occasional brusqueness of her manner and the fruity names she sees fit to call me from time to time, she loves me dearly and my well-being is very near her heart.

"She's pretty highbrow for you, isn't she? If I know her, she'll have you reading W. H. Auden before you can say 'What ho.'"

"She rather hinted at some such contingency, though, if I recollect, T. S. Eliot was the name that was mentioned."

"She proposes to mold you?"

"I gathered so."

"You won't like that."

"No."

She nodded understandingly.

"Men don't. I attribute my own happy marriage to the fact that I have never so much as laid a finger on old Tom. Agatha is trying to mold Worplesdon, and I believe his agonies are frightful. She made him knock off smoking the other day, and he behaved like a cinnamon bear with its foot in a trap. Has Florence told you to knock off smoking?"

"Not yet."

"She will. And after that it'll be cocktails." She gazed at me with a good deal of what-do-you-call-it. You could see that remorse had her in its grip. "I'm afraid I've got you into a bit of a jam, my poppet."

"Don't give it a thought, old blood relation," I said. "These things happen. It is your predicament, not mine, that is exercising me. We've got to get you out of your sea of troubles, as Jeeves calls it. Everything else is relatively unimportant. My thoughts of self are merely in about the proportion of the vermouth to the gin in a strongish dry martini."

She was plainly touched. Unless I am very much mistaken, her eyes were wet with unshed tears.

"That's very altruistic of you, Bertie dear."

"Not at all, not at all."

"One wouldn't think it, to look at you, but you have a noble soul."

"*Who* wouldn't think it, to look at me?"

"And if that's the way you feel, all I can say is that it does you credit and let's get going. You'd better go and shift that ladder to the right window."

"You mean the left window."

"Well, let's call it the correct window."

I braced myself to break the bad news.

"Ah," I said, "but what you're overlooking—possibly because I forgot to tell you—is that a snag has arisen which threatens to do our aims and objects a bit of no good. The ladder isn't there."

"Where?"

"Under the right window, or perhaps I should say the wrong window. When I looked out, it was gone."

"Nonsense. Ladders don't melt into thin air."

"They do, I assure you, at Brinkley Court, Brinkley-cum-Snodsfield-in-the-Marsh. I don't know what conditions prevail elsewhere, but at Brinkley Court they vanish if you take your eye off them for so much as an instant."

"You mean the ladder's disappeared?"

"That is precisely the point I was endeavoring to establish. It has folded its tents like the Arabs and silently stolen away."

She turned bright mauve, and I think was about to rap

out something in the nature of a Quorn-and-Pytchley expletive, for she is a woman who seldom minces her words when stirred, but at this juncture the door opened and Uncle Tom came in. I was too distrait to be able to discern whether or not he was pottering, but a glance was enough to show me that he was definitely all of a doddah.

"Dahlia!" he exclaimed. "I thought I heard your voice. What are you doing up at this hour?"

"Bertie had a headache," replied the old relative, a quick thinker. "I have been giving him an aspirin. The head a little better now, Bertie?"

"One notes a slight improvement," I assured her, being a quick thinker myself. "You're out and about a bit late, aren't you, Uncle Tom?"

"Yes," said Aunt Dahlia. "What are *you* doing up at this hour, my old for-better-and-for-worser? You ought to have been asleep ages ago."

Uncle Tom shook his head. His air was grave.

"Asleep, old girl? I shan't get any sleep tonight. Far too worried. The place is alive with burglars."

"Burglars? What gives you that idea? I haven't seen any burglars. Have you, Bertie?"

"Not one. I remember thinking how odd it was."

"You probably saw an owl or something, Tom."

"I saw a ladder. When I was taking my stroll in the garden before going to bed. Propped up against one of the windows. I took it away in the nick of time. A minute later, and burglars would have been streaming up it in their thousands."

Aunt Dahlia and I exchanged a glance. I think we were both feeling happier now that the mystery of the vanishing l. had been solved. It's an odd thing, but however much of an aficionado one may be of mysteries in book form, when they pop up in real life they seldom fail to give one the pip.

She endeavored to soothe his agitation.

"Probably just a ladder one of the gardeners was using and forgot to put back where it belonged. Though, of course," she went on thoughtfully, feeling no doubt that a spot of paving the way would do no harm, "I suppose there is always a chance of a cracksman having a try for that valuable pearl necklace of mine. I had forgotten that."

"I hadn't," said Uncle Tom. "It was the first thing I thought of. I went straight to your room and got it and locked it up in the safe in the hall. A burglar will have to be pretty smart to get it out of there," he added with modest pride, and pushed off, leaving behind him what I have sometimes heard called a pregnant silence.

Aunt looked at nephew, nephew looked at aunt.

"Hell's whiskers!" said the former, starting the conversation going again. "Now what do we do?"

I agreed that the situation was sticky. Indeed, offhand it was difficult to see how it could have been more glutinous.

"What are the chances of finding out the combination?"

"Not a hope."

"I wonder if Jeeves can crack a safe."

She brightened.

"I'll bet he can. There's nothing Jeeves can't do. Go and fetch him."

I Lord-love-a-duck-ed impatiently.

"How the dickens can I fetch him? I don't know which his room is. Do you?"

"No."

"Well, I can't go from door to door, rousing the whole domestic staff. Who do you think I am? Paul Revere?"

I paused for a reply, and as I did so who should come in

but Jeeves in person. Late though it was, the hour had produced the man.

"Excuse me, sir," he said. "I am happy to find that I have not interrupted your slumbers. I ventured to come to inquire whether matters had developed satisfactorily. Were you successful in your enterprise, sir?"

I shook the cocoanut.

"No, Jeeves. I moved in a mysterious way my wonders to perform, but was impeded by a number of Acts of God," I said, and in a few crisp words put him abreast. "So the necklace is now in the safe," I concluded, "and the problem as I see it, and as Aunt Dahlia sees it, is how the dickens to get it out. You grasp the position?"

"Yes, sir. It is disturbing."

Aunt Dahlia uttered a passionate cry.

"Don't *do* it!" she boomed with extraordinary vehemence. "If I hear that word 'disturbing' once more . . . Can you bust a safe, Jeeves?"

"No, madam."

"Don't say 'No, madam' in that casual way. How do you know you can't?"

"It requires a specialized education and upbringing, madam."

"Then I'm for it," said Aunt Dahlia, making for the door. Her face was grim and set. She might have been a marquise about to hop into the tumbril at the time when there was all that unpleasantness over in France. "You weren't through the San Francisco earthquake, were you, Jeeves?"

"No, madam. I have never visited the western coastal towns of the United States."

"I was only thinking that if you had been, what's going to happen tomorrow when this Lord Sidcup arrives and tells Tom the awful truth would have reminded you of old times. Well, good night, all. I'll be running along and getting my beauty sleep."

She buzzed off, a gallant figure. The Quorn trains its daughters well. No weakness there. In the fell clutch of circumstance, as I remember Jeeves putting it once, they do not wince or cry aloud. I mentioned this to him as the door closed, and he agreed that it was substantially so.

"Under the tiddly-poms of whatever-it-is . . . How does the rest of it go?"

"Under the bludgeonings of chance their heads are . . . pardon me . . . bloody but unbowed, sir."

"That's right. Your own?"

"No, sir. The late William Ernest Henley, 1849–1903."

"Ah?"

"The title of the poem is 'Invictus.' But did I understand Mrs. Travers to say that Lord Sidcup was expected, sir?"

"He arrives tomorrow."

"Would he be the gentleman of whom you were speaking, who is to examine Mrs. Travers's necklace?"

"That's the chap."

"Then I fancy that all is well, sir."

I started. It seemed to me that I must have misunderstood him. Either that, or he was talking through his hat.

"All is *well*, did you say, Jeeves?"

"Yes, sir. You are not aware who Lord Sidcup is, sir?"

"I never heard of him in my life."

"You will possibly remember him, sir, as Mr. Roderick Spode."

I stared at him. You could have knocked me down with a toothpick.

"Roderick Spode?"

"Yes, sir."

"You mean the Roderick Spode of Totleigh Towers?"

"Precisely, sir. He recently succeeded to the title on the demise of the late Lord Sidcup, his uncle."

"Great Scott, Jeeves!"

"Yes, sir. I think you will agree with me, sir, that in these circumstances the problem confronting Mrs. Travers is susceptible of a ready solution. A word to his lordship, reminding him of the fact that he sells ladies' underclothing under the trade name of Eulalie Soeurs, should go far towards inducing him to preserve a tactful silence with regard to the spurious nature of the necklace. At the time of our visit to Totleigh Towers you will recollect that Mr. Spode, as he then was, showed unmistakably his reluctance to let the matter become generally known."

"Egad, Jeeves!"

"Yes, sir. I thought I would mention it, sir. Good night, sir."

He oozed off.

15

WE WOOSTERS are never very early risers, and the sun was highish in the heavens next morning when I woke to greet a new day. And I had just finished tucking away a refreshing scrambled eggs and coffee, when the door opened as if a hurricane had hit it and Aunt Dahlia came pirouetting in.

I use the word "pirouetting" advisedly, for there was an elasticity in her bearing which impressed itself immediately upon the eye. Of the drooping mourner of last night there remained no trace. The woman was plainly right above herself.

"Bertie," she said, after a brief opening speech in the course of which she described me as a lazy young hound who ought to be ashamed to be wallowing in bed on what, if you asked her, was the maddest merriest day of all the glad new year, "I've just been talking to Jeeves, and if ever a lifesaving friend in need drew breath, it is he. Hats off to Jeeves is the way I look at it."

Pausing for a moment to voice the view that my moustache was an offense against God and man but that she saw in it nothing that a good weed-killer couldn't cure, she resumed.

"He tells me this Lord Sidcup who's coming here today is none other than our old pal Roderick Spode."

I nodded. I had divined from her exuberance that he must have been spilling the big news.

"Correct," I said. "Apparently, all unknown to us, Spode was right from the start the secret nephew of the holder of the title, and since that sojourn of ours at Totleigh Towers the latter has gone to reside with the morning stars, giving him a stepup. Jeeves has also, I take it, told you about Eulalie Soeurs?"

"The whole thing. Why didn't you ever let me in on that? You know how I enjoy a good laugh."

I spread the hands in a dignified gesture, upsetting the coffee pot, which was fortunately empty.

"My lips were sealed."

"You and your lips!"

"All right, me and my lips. But I repeat. The information was imparted to me in confidence."

"You could have told Auntie."

I shook my head. Women do not understand these things. *Noblesse oblige* means nothing to the gentler sex.

"One does not impart confidential confidences even to Auntie, not if one is a confidant of the right sort."

"Well, anyway, I now have the facts, and I hold Spode, alias Sidcup, in the hollow of my hand. Bless my soul," she went on, a far-off ecstatic look on her face, "how well I remember that day at Totleigh Towers. There he was, advancing on you with glittering eyes and foam-flecked lips, and you drew yourself up as cool as some cucumbers, as Anatole would say, and said 'One minute, Spode, just one minute. It may interest you to learn that I know all about Eulalie.' Gosh, how I admired you!"

"I don't wonder."

"You were like one of those lion tamers in circuses who defy murderous man-eating monarchs of the jungle."

"There was a resemblance, no doubt."

"And how he wilted! I've never seen anything like it. Before my eyes he wilted like a wet sock. And he's going to do it again when he gets here this evening."

"You propose to draw him aside and tell him you know his guilty secret?"

"Exactly. Strongly recommending him, when Tom shows him the necklace, to say it's a lovely bit of work and worth every penny he paid for it. It can't fail. Fancy him owning Eulalie Soeurs! He must make a packet out of it. I was in there last month, buying some cami-knickers, and the place was doing a roaring trade. Money pouring in like a tidal wave. By the way, laddie, talking of cami-knickers, Florence was showing me hers just now. Not the ones she had on, I don't mean, her reserve supply. She wanted my opinion of them. And I'm sorry to tell you, my poor lamb," she said, eyeing me with auntly pity, "that things look pretty serious in that quarter."

"They do?"

"Extremely serious. She's all set to start those wedding bells ringing out. Somewhere around next November, she seems to think, at St. George's, Hanover Square. Already she is speaking freely of bridesmaids and caterers." She paused, and looked at me in a surprised sort of way. "You don't seem very upset," she said. "Are you one of these men of chilled steel one reads about?"

I spread the hands again, this time without disaster to the breakfast tray.

"Well, I'll tell you, old ancestor. When a fellow has been engaged as often as I have and each time saved from the scaffold at the eleventh hour, he comes to have faith in his star. He feels that all is not lost till they have actually got him at the altar rails with the organ playing 'Oh, Perfect Love' and the clergyman saying 'Wilt thou?' At the moment, admittedly, I am in the soup, but it may well be that in God's good time it will be granted to me to emerge unscathed from the tureen."

"You don't despair?"

"Not at all. I have high hopes that, after they have thought things over, these two proud spirits who have parted brass rags will come together and be reconciled, thus letting me out. The rift was due—"

"I know. She told me."

"—to the fact that Stilton learned that I had taken Florence to The Mottled Oyster one night about a week ago, and he refused to believe that I had done so merely in order to enable her to accumulate atmosphere for her new book. When he has cooled off and reason has returned to its throne, he may realize how mistaken he was and beg her to forgive him for his low suspicions. I think so. I hope so."

She agreed that there was something in this and commended me for my spirit, which in her opinion was the right one. My intrepidity reminded her, she said, of the Spartans at Thermopylae, wherever that may be.

"But he's a long way from being in that frame of mind at the moment, according to Florence. She says he is convinced that you two were on an unbridled toot together. And, of course, his finding you in the cupboard in her bedroom at one in the morning was unfortunate."

"Most. One would gladly have avoided the occurrence."

"Must have given the man quite a start. What beats me is why he didn't hammer the stuffing out of you. I should have thought that would have been his first move."

I smiled quietly.

"He has drawn me in the Drones Club Darts sweep."

"What's that got to do with it?"

"My dear old soul, does a fellow hammer the stuffing out of a chap on whose virtuosity at the Darts board he stands to win fifty-six pounds, ten shillings?"

"Oh, I see."

"So did Stilton. I made the position thoroughly clear to him, and he has ceased to be a menace. However much his thoughts may drift in the direction of stuffing-hammering, he will have to continue to maintain the non-belligerent status of a mild cat in an adage. I have bottled him up good and proper. There was nothing further you wished to discuss?"

"Not that I know of."

"Then if you will withdraw, I will be getting up and dressing."

I rose from the hay as the door closed, and having bathed, shaved, and clad the outer man, took my cigarette out for a stroll in the grounds and messuages.

The sun was now a good bit higher in the heavens than when last observed, and its genial warmth increased the optimism of my mood. Thinking of Stilton and the dead stymie I had laid him, I found myself feeling that it was not such a bad little old world, after all. I don't know anything that braces you more thoroughly than outgeneraling one of the baser sort who has been chucking his weight about and planning to start something. It was with much the same quiet satisfaction which I had experienced when bending Roderick Spode to my will at Totleigh Towers that I contemplated Stilton in his bottled-up state. As Aunt Dahlia had said, quite the lion tamer.

True, as against this, there was Florence—already, it appeared, speaking freely of bridesmaids, caterers, and

St. George's, Hanover Square—and a lesser man might have allowed her dark shadow to cloud his feeling of *bien être*. But it is always the policy of the Woosters to count their blessings one by one, and I concentrated my attention exclusively on the bright side of the picture, telling myself that even if an eleventh hour reprieve failed to materialize and I was compelled to drain the bitter cup, I wouldn't have to do it with two black eyes and a fractured spine, wedding presents from G. D'Arcy Cheesewright. Come what might, I was that much ahead of the game.

I was, in short, in buoyant mood and practically saying "Tra la," when I observed Jeeves shimmering up in the manner of one desiring audience.

"Ah, Jeeves," I said. "Nice morning."

"Extremely agreeable, sir."

"Did you want to see me about something?"

"If you could spare me a moment, sir. I was anxious to ascertain if it would be possible for you to dispense with my services today in order that I may go to London. The Junior Ganymede luncheon, sir."

"I thought that was next week."

"The date has been put forward to accommodate Sir Everard Everett's butler, who leaves with his employer tomorrow for the United States of America. Sir Everard is assuming his duties as Britannic ambassador at Washington."

"Is that so? Good luck to the old blister."

"Yes, sir."

"One likes to see these public servants bustling about and earning their salaries."

"Yes, sir."

"If one is a taxpayer, I mean, contributing one's whack to those salaries."

"Precisely, sir. I should be glad if you could see your way to allowing me to attend the function, sir. As I informed you, I am taking the chair."

Well, of course, when he puts it like that, I had no option but to right-ho.

"Certainly, Jeeves. Push along and revel till your ribs squeak. It may be your last chance," I added significantly.

"Sir?"

"Well, you've often stressed how fussy the brass hats are about members not revealing the secrets of the club book, and Aunt Dahlia tells me you've just been spilling the whole inner history of Spode and Eulalie Soeurs to her. Won't they drum you out if this becomes known?"

"The contingency is a remote one, sir, and I gladly took the risk, knowing that Mrs. Travers's happiness was at stake."

"Pretty white, Jeeves."

"Thank you, sir. I endeavor to give satisfaction. And now I think perhaps, if you will excuse me, sir, I should be starting for the station. The train for London leaves very shortly."

"Why not drive up in the two-seater?"

"If you could spare it, sir?"

"Of course."

"Thank you very much, sir. It will be a great convenience."

He pushed off in the direction of the house, no doubt to go and get the bowler hat which is his inseparable companion when in the metropolis, and scarcely had he left me when I heard my name called in a bleating voice and turned to perceive Percy Gorringe approaching, his tortoiseshell-rimmed spectacles glistening in the sunshine.

My first emotion on beholding him was one of surprise, a feeling that of all the in and out performers I had ever met he was the most unpredictable. I mean, you couldn't tell from one minute to another what aspect he was going to present to the world, for he switched from Stormy to Set Fair and from Set Fair to Stormy like a barometer with something wrong with its works. At dinner on the previous night he had been all gaiety and effervescence, and here he was now, only a few hours later, once more giving that impersonation of a dead codfish which had caused Aunt Dahlia to take so strong a line with him. Fixing me with lack-luster eyes, if lack-luster is the word I want, and wasting no time on preliminary pip-pippings and *pourparlers,* he started straight off cleansing his bosom of the perilous stuff that weighs upon the heart.

"Wooster," he said, "Florence has just told me a story that shocked me!"

Well, difficult to know what to say to that, of course. One's impulse was to ask what story, adding that if it was the one about the bishop and the lady snake charmer, one had heard it. And one could, no doubt, have shoved in a thoughtful word or two deploring the growing laxity of speech of the modern girl. I merely said "Oh, ah?" and waited for further details.

His eye, as Florence's had done on the previous night, rolled in a fine frenzy and glanced from heaven to earth, from earth to heaven. You could see the thing had upset him.

"Shortly after breakfast," he continued, retrieving the eye and fixing it on me once more, "finding her alone in the herbaceous border, cutting flowers, I hastened up and asked if I might be allowed to hold the basket."

"Very civil."

"She thanked me and said she would be glad if I would do so, and for awhile we talked of neutral subjects. One topic led to another, and eventually I asked her to be my wife."

"'At-a-boy!'"

"I beg your pardon?"

"I only said ''At-a-boy!'"

"Why did you say ''At-a-boy!'?"

"Sort of cheering you on, as it were."

"I see. Cheering me on. The expression is a corruption, one assumes, of the phrase 'That is the boy' and signifies friendly encouragement?"

"That's right."

"Then I am surprised in the circumstances—and may I say more than a little disgusted—to hear it from your lips, Wooster. It would have been in better taste to have refrained from cheap taunts and jeers."

"Eh?"

"If you have triumphed, that is no reason why you should mock those who have been less fortunate."

"I'm sorry. If you could give me a few footnotes . . ."

He tchah-ed impatiently.

"I told you that I asked Florence to be my wife, and I also told you that she said something which shocked me profoundly. It was that she was engaged to you."

I got it now. I saw what he was driving at.

"Oh, ah, yes, of course. Quite. Yes, we would appear to be betrothed."

"When did this happen, Wooster?"

"Fairly recently."

He snorted.

"Very recently, I should imagine, seeing that it was only yesterday that she was engaged to Cheesewright. It's all most confusing," said Percy peevishly. "It makes one's head swim. One doesn't know where one is."

I could see his point.

"Bit of a mixup," I agreed.

"It's bewildering. I cannot think what she can possibly see in you."

"No. Very odd, the whole thing."

He brooded darkly awhile.

"Her recent infatuation for Cheesewright," he said, teeing off again, "one could dimly understand. Whatever his mental defects, he is a vigorous young animal, and it is not uncommon to find girls of intellect attracted by vigorous young animals. Bernard Shaw made this the basis of his early novel, *Cashel Byron's Profession.* But *you*! It's inexplicable. A mere weedy butterfly."

"Would you call me a weedy butterfly?"

"If you can think of a better description, I shall be happy to hear it. I am unable to discern in you the slightest vestige of charm, the smallest trace of any quality that could reasonably be expected to appeal to a girl like Florence. It amazes one that she should wish to have you permanently about the house."

I don't know if you would call me a touchy man. As a rule, I should say not. But it is not pleasant to find yourself chalked upon the slate as a weedy butterfly, and I confess that I spoke a little shortly.

"Well, there it is," I said, and went into the silence. And as he, too, seemed disinclined for chit-chat, we stood for some moments like a couple of Trappist monks who have run into each other by chance at the dog races. And I think I would pretty soon have nodded curtly and removed myself, had he not arrested me with an exclamation similar in tone and volume to the one which Stilton had uttered on finding me festooned with hat boxes in Florence's cupboard. He was looking at me through the windshields with what appeared to be concern, if not horror. It puzzled me. It couldn't have taken him all this time, I felt, to notice the moustache.

"Wooster! Good gracious! You are not wearing a hat!"

"I don't much in the country."

"But in this hot sun! You might get sunstroke. You ought not to take such risks."

I must say I was touched by this solicitude. Much of the pique I had been feeling left me. It isn't many fellows, I mean to say, who get all worked up about the well-being of birds who are virtually strangers. It just showed, I thought, that a man may talk a lot of rot about weedy butterflies and still have a tender heart beneath what I should imagine was pretty generally recognized as a fairly repulsive exterior.

"Don't worry," I said, soothing his alarm.

"But I do worry," he responded sharply. "I feel very strongly that you ought either to get a hat or else stay in the shade. I don't want to appear fussy, but your health is naturally a matter of greatest concern to me. You see, I have drawn you in the Drones Club Darts sweep."

This got right past me. I could make nothing of it. It sounded to me like straight delirium.

"You've what? How do you mean you've drawn me in the Drones Club Darts sweep?"

"I put it badly. I was agitated. What I should have said was that I have bought you from Cheesewright. He has sold me the ticket bearing your name. So can you wonder that it makes me nervous when I see you going about in this hot sun without a hat?"

In a career liberally spotted with nasty shocks I have

had occasion to do quite a bit of reeling and tottering from time to time, but I have seldom reeled and tottered more heartily than I did on hearing these frightful words. I had addressed Aunt Dahlia earlier in the morning, if you remember, as a fluttering aspen. The description would have fitted me at this moment like the paper on the wall.

This surge of emotion will, I think, be readily understood. My whole foreign policy, as I have made clear, had been built on the fact that I had bottled Stilton up good and proper, and it now appeared, dash it, that I hadn't bottled him up at all. He was once more in the position of an Assyrian fully licensed to come down like a wolf on the fold with his cohorts all gleaming with purple and gold, and the realization that his thirst for vengeance was so pronounced that, rather than forgo his war aims, he was prepared to sacrifice fifty-six quid and a bender was one that froze the marrow.

"There must be a lot of hidden good in Cheesewright," proceeded Percy. "I confess frankly that I misjudged him, and if I had not already returned the galley proofs, I would withdraw that 'Caliban at Sunset' thing of mine from *Parnassus*. He tells me that you are a certain winner of this Darts contest, and yet he voluntarily offered to sell me for quite a trivial sum the ticket bearing your name, because, he said, he had taken a great fancy to me and would like to do me a good turn. A big, generous, warmhearted gesture, and one that restores one's faith in human nature. By the way, Cheesewright is looking for you. He wants to see you about something."

He repeated his advice with ref. to the hat and moved off, and for quite awhile I stood where I was, rigid to the last limb, my numbed bean trying to grapple with this hideous problem which had arisen. It was plain that some diabolically clever countermove would have to be made and made slippily, but what diabolically clever countermove? There was what is called the rub.

You see, it wasn't as if I could just leg it from the danger zone, which was what I would have liked to do. It was imperative that I be among those present at Brinkley Court when Spode arrived this evening. Airily though Aunt Dahlia had spoken of making the man play ball, it was quite conceivable that the program might blow a fuse, in which event the presence on the spot of a quick-thinking nephew would be of the essence. The Woosters do not desert aunts in the time of need.

Eliminating, therefore, the wings of the dove, for which I would gladly have been in the market, what other course presented itself? I freely own that for five minutes or so the thing had me snookered.

But it has often been said of Bertram Wooster that in moments of intense peril he has an uncanny knack of getting inspiration, and this happened now. Suddenly a thought came like a full-blown rose, flushing the brow, and I picked up the feet and lit out for the stables, where my two-seater was housed. It might be that Jeeves had not yet started on the long trail that led to the Junior Ganymede Club, and if he hadn't, I saw the way out.

16

IF YOU ARE one of the better element who are never happier than when curled up with the works of B. Wooster, you possibly came across a previous slab of these reminiscences of mine in which I dealt with a visit Jeeves and I paid to Deverill Hall, the rural seat of Esmond Haddock, J.P., and will recall that while under the Haddock roof Jeeves found my Aunt Agatha's son Thos in possession of what is known as a cosh and very prudently impounded it, feeling—as who wouldn't—that it was the last thing that ought to be at the disposal of that homicidal young thug. The thought which had flushed my brow in the manner described was . . . Had Jeeves still got it? Everything turned on that.

I found him, richly appareled and wearing the bowler hat, at the wheel of the car, on the point of putting foot to self-starter. Another moment, and I should have been too late. Racing up, I inaugurated the quiz without delay.

"Jeeves," I said, "throw your mind back to that time we stayed at Deverill Hall. Are you throwing?"

"Yes, sir."

"Then continue to follow me closely. My Aunt Agatha's son, young Thos, was there."

"Precisely, sir."

"With the idea of employing it on a schoolmate of his called Stinker, who had incurred his displeasure for some reason, he had purchased before leaving London a cosh."

"Or blackjack, to use the American term."

"Never mind American terms, Jeeves. You took the weapon from him."

"I deemed it wisest, sir."

"It was wisest. No argument about that. Let a plug-ugly like young Thos loose in the community with a cosh, and you are inviting disasters and . . . what's the word? Something about cats."

"Cataclysms, sir?"

"That's it. Cataclysms. Unquestionably you did the right thing. But all that is beside the point. What I am leading up to is this. That cosh, where is it?"

"Among my effects at the apartment, sir."

"I'll drive with you to London and pick it up."

"I could bring it with me on my return, sir."

I did a brief dance step. On his return, forsooth! When would that be? Late at night, probably, because the gang at a hot spot like the Junior Ganymede don't break up a party at the end of lunch. I know what happens when these wild butlers let themselves go. They sit around till all hours, drinking deep and singing close harmony and generally whooping it up like a bunch of the boys at the Malemute saloon. It would mean that for the whole of the long summer day I should be defenseless, an easy prey for a Stilton who, as I had just been informed, was prowling about, seeking whom he might devour.

"That's no good, Jeeves. I require it immediately. Not tonight, not a week from Wednesday, but at the earliest possible moment. I am being hotly pursued by Cheesewright, Jeeves."

"Indeed, sir?"

"And if I am to stave off the Cheesewright challenge, I shall have need of a weapon. His strength is as the strength of ten, and unarmed I should be corn before his sickle."

"Extremely well put, sir, if I may say so, and your diagnosis of the situation is perfectly accurate. Mr. Cheesewright's robustness would enable him to crush you like a fly."

"Exactly."

"He would obliterate you with a single blow. He would break you in two with his bare hands. He would tear you limb from limb."

I frowned slightly. I was glad to see that he appreciated the gravity of the situation, but these crude physical details seemed to me uncalled for.

"No need to make a production number of it, Jeeves," I said with a touch of coldness. "What I am driving at is that, armed with the cosh, I can face the blighter without a tremor. You agree?"

"Most decidedly, sir."

"Then shift-ho," I said, and hurled myself into the vacant seat.

This cosh of which I have been speaking was a small rubber bludgeon which at first sight you might have supposed unequal to the task of coping with an adversary of Stilton Cheesewright's tonnage. In repose, I mean to say, it didn't look like anything so frightfully hot. But I had seen it in action and was hep to what Florence would have called its latent potentialities. At Deverill Hall one night, for the soundest of reasons but too long to go into here, Jeeves had had occasion to bean a policeman with it— Constable Dobbs, a zealous officer—and the smitten slop had dropped as the gentle rain from heaven upon the place beneath.

There is a song, frequently sung by curates at village concerts, which runs:

> *I fear no foe in shining armor,*
> *Though his lance be bright and keen.*

Or is it "swift and keen"? I can't remember. Not that it matters. The point is that those words summed up my attitude to a nicety. They put what I was feeling in a nutshell. With that cosh on my person, I should feel debonair and confident, no matter how many Cheesewrights came bounding at me with slavering jaws.

Everything went according to plan. After an agreeable drive we dropped anchor at the door of Berkeley Mansions and made our way to the flat. There, as foreshadowed, was the cosh. Jeeves handed it over, I thanked him in a few well-chosen words, he went off to his orgy, and I, after a bite of lunch at the Drones, settled myself in the two-seater and turned its nose Worcestershirewards.

The first person I met as I passed through the portals of Brinkley Court some hours later was Aunt Dahlia. She was in the hall, pacing up and down like a distraught tigress. Her exuberance of the morning had vanished completely, leaving her once more the haggard aunt of yesterday, and I was conscious of a quick pang of concern.

"Golly!" I said. "What's up, old relative? Don't tell me that scheme of yours didn't work?"

She kicked morosely at a handy chair, sending it flying into the unknown.

"It hasn't had a chance to work."

"Why not? Didn't Spode turn up?"

She gazed about her with somber eyes, apparently in the hope of finding another chair to kick. There not being one in her immediate sphere of influence, she kicked the sofa.

"He turned up all right, and what happened? Before I could draw him aside and get so much as a word in, Tom swooped on him and took him off to the collection room to look at his foul silver. They've been in there for more than an hour, and how much longer they're going to be, Heaven knows."

I pursed the lips. One ought, I felt, to have anticipated something of this sort.

"Can't you detach him?"

"No human power can detach a man to whom Tom is talking about his silver collection. He holds him with a glittering eye. All I can hope is that he will be so wrapped up in the silver end of the thing that he'll forget all about the necklace."

The last thing a nephew of the right sort wants to do is to shove a wallowing aunt still more deeply beneath the surface of the slough of despond than she is already, but I had to shake my head at this.

"I doubt it."

She gave the sofa another juicy one.

"So do I doubt it. That's why I'm going steadily cuckoo and may at any moment start howling like a banshee. Sooner or later he'll remember to take Spode to the safe, and what I am saying to myself is When? When? I feel like . . . who was the man who sat with a sword dangling over him, suspended by a hair, wondering how long it was going to be before it dropped and gave him a nasty flesh wound?"

She had me there. Nobody I had met. Certainly not one of the fellows at the Drones, or I should have heard about it.

"I couldn't tell you, I'm afraid. Jeeves might know."

At the mention of that honored name her eyes lit up.

"Jeeves! Of course! He's the man I want. Where is he?"

"In London. He asked me if he could take the day off. It was the Junior Ganymede monthly luncheon today."

She uttered a cry which might have been the howl of the banshee to which she had alluded, and gave me the sort of look which in the old tally-ho days she would have given a mentally deficient hound which she had observed suspending its professional activities in order to chase a rabbit.

"You let Jeeves go away at a time like this, when one has never needed him more?"

"I hadn't the heart to refuse. He was taking the chair. He'll be back soon."

"By which time . . ."

She would have spoken further . . . a good deal further, if I read aright the message in her eyes . . . but before she could get going something whiskered came down the stairs and Percy was with us.

Seeing me, he halted abruptly.

"Wooster!" His agitation was very marked. "Where have you been all day, Wooster?"

I told him I had driven to London, and he drew his breath in with a hiss.

"In this hot weather? It can't be good for you. You must not overtax yourself, Wooster. You must husband your strength."

He had chosen the wrong moment for horning in. The old relative turned on him as if he had been someone she had observed heading off the fox, if not shooting it.

"Gorringe, you ghastly sheepfaced fugitive from hell," she thundered, forgetting, or so I imagine, that she was a hostess, "get out of here, blast you. We're in conference."

I suppose mixing with editors of poetry magazines toughens a fellow, rendering him impervious to verbal assault, for Percy, who might well have been expected to wilt, didn't wilt by a damn sight but drew himself up to his full height, which was about six feet two, and came back at her strongly.

"I am sorry to have intruded at an unseasonable moment, Mrs. Travers," he said, with a simple dignity that became him well, "but I have a message for you from Moth-aw, Moth-aw would like to speak to you. She desired me to ask if it would be convenient if she came to your room."

Aunt Dahlia flung her hands up emotionally. I could understand how she felt. The last thing a woman wants, when distraught, is a chat with someone like Ma Trotter.

"Not now!"

"Later, perhaps?"

"Is it important?"

"I received the impression that it was most important."

Aunt Dahlia heaved a deep sigh, the sigh of a woman who feels that they are coming over the plate too fast for her.

"Oh, all right. Tell her I'll see her in half an hour. I'm going back to the collection room, Bertie. It's just possible that Tom may have run down by now. But one last word," she added, as she moved away. "The next subhuman gargoyle that comes butting in and distracting my thoughts when I am trying to wrestle with vital problems takes his life in his hands. Let him make his will and put in his order for lilies!"

She disappeared at some forty m.p.h., and Percy followed her retreating form with an indulgent eye.

"A quaint character," he said.

I agreed that the old relative was quaint in spots.

"She reminds me a little of the editress of *Parnassus*. The same tendency to wave her hands and shout, when stirred. But about this drive of yours to London, Wooster. What made you go there?"

"Oh, just one or two things I had to attend to."

"Well, I am thankful that you got back safely. The toll of the roads is so high these days. I trust you always drive carefully, Wooster? No speeding? No passing on blind corners? Capital, capital. But we were all quite anxious about you. We couldn't think where you could have got to. Cheesewright was particularly concerned. He appeared to think that you had vanished permanently and he said there were all sorts of things he had been hoping to discuss with you. I must let him know you are back. It will relieve his mind."

He trotted off, and I lit a nonchalant cigarette, calm and collected to the eyebrows. I was perhaps halfway through it and had just blown quite a goodish smoke ring, when clumping footsteps made themselves heard and Stilton loomed up on the skyline.

I reached a hand into my pocket and got a firm grasp on the old Equalizer.

17

I DON'T KNOW if you have ever seen a tiger of the jungle drawing a deep breath preparatory to doing a swan dive and landing with both feet on the backbone of one of the minor fauna. Probably not, nor, as a matter of fact, have I. But I should imagine that a t. of the j. at such a moment would look . . . allowing, of course, for the fact that it would not have a pink face and a head like a pumpkin . . . exactly as G. D'Arcy Cheesewright looked as his eyes rested on the Wooster frame. For perhaps a couple of ticks he stood there inflating and deflating his chest. Then he said, as I had rather supposed he would:

"Ho!"

His signature tune, as you might say.

My nonchalance continued undiminished. It would have been idle to pretend that the blister's attitude was not menacing. It was about as menacing as it could jolly well stick. But with my hand on the cosh I faced him without a tremor. Like Caesar's wife, I was ready for anything.

I gave him a careless nod.

"Ah, Stilton," I said. "How are tricks?"

The question appeared to set the seal on his hotted-up-ness. He gnashed a tooth or two.

"I'll show you how tricks are! I've been looking for you all day."

"You wished to see me about something?"

"I wished to pull your head off at the roots and make you swallow it."

I nodded again, carelessly as before.

"Ah, yes. You rather hinted at some such desire last night, did you not? It all comes back to me. Well, I'm sorry, Stilton, but I'm afraid it's off. I have made other plans. Percy Gorringe will no doubt have told you that I ran up to London this morning. I went to get this," I said, and producing the man of slender physique's best friend, gave it a suggestive waggle.

There is one drawback to not wearing a moustache, and that is that if you don't have one, you've got nothing to twirl when baffled. All you can do is stand with your lower jaw drooping like a tired lily, looking a priceless ass, and that is what Stilton was doing now. His whole demeanor was that of an Assyrian who, having come down like a wolf on the fold, finds in residence not lambs but wildcats, than which, of course, nothing makes an Assyrian feel sillier.

"Amazingly effective little contrivances, these," I proceeded, rubbing it in. "You read about them a good deal in mystery thrillers. Coshes they are called, though blackjack is, I believe, the American term."

He breathed stertorously, his eyes bulging. I suppose he had never come up against anything like this before. One gets new experiences.

"You put that thing down!" he said hoarsely.

"I propose to put it down," I replied, quick as a flash. "I propose to put it down jolly dashed hard, the moment you make a move, and though I am the merest novice in the use of the cosh, I don't see how I can help hitting a head the size of yours somewhere. And then where will you be, Cheesewright? On the floor, dear old soul, that's where you will be, with me carelessly dusting my hands and putting the instrument back in my pocket. With one of these things in his possession the veriest weakling can lay out the toughest egg colder than a halibut on ice. To put it in a word, Cheesewright, I am armed, and the setup, as I see it, is this. I take a comfortable stance with the weight balanced on both feet, you make a spring, and I, cool as some cucumbers . . ."

It was a silly thing to say, that about making springs, because it put ideas into his head. He made one on the word "cucumbers" with such abruptness that I was caught completely unawares. That's the trouble with beefy fellows like Stilton. They are so massive that you don't credit them with the ability to get off the mark like jack rabbits and fly through the air with the greatest of ease. Before I knew what had happened, the cosh, wrenched from my grasp, was sailing across the hall, to come to rest on the floor near Uncle Tom's safe.

I stood there defenseless.

Well, "stood" is putting it loosely. In crises like this we Woosters do not stand. It was soon made abundantly clear that Stilton was not the only one of our little circle who could get off marks like jack rabbits. I doubt if in the whole of Australia, where this species of animal abounds, you could have found a jack rabbit capable of a tithe of the swift smoothness with which I removed myself from the pulsating center of things. To do a backward jump of some eleven feet and install myself behind the sofa was with me the work of an instant, and there for awhile the matter rested, because every time he came charging round to my side like a greyhound I went whizzing round to his side like an electric hare, rendering his every effort null and void. Those great Generals, of whom I was speaking earlier, go in for this maneuver quite a bit. Strategic redeployment is the technical term.

How long this round-and-round-the-mulberry-bush sequence would have continued, it is not easy to say, but probably not any great length of time, for already my partner in the rhythmic doings was beginning to show signs of feeling the pace. Stilton, like so many of these beefy birds, is apt, when not in training for some aquatic contest, to yield to the lure of the fleshpots. This takes its toll. By the end of the first dozen laps, while I remained as fresh as a daisy, prepared to fight it out on this line if it took all summer, he was puffing quite considerably and his brow had become wet with honest sweat.

But, as so often happens on these occasions, the fixture was not played to a finish. Pausing for a moment before starting on lap thirteen, we were interrupted by the entry of Seppings, Aunt Dahlia's butler, who came toddling in, looking rather official.

I was glad to see him myself, for some sort of interruption was just what I had been hoping for, but this turning of the thing into a threesome plainly displeased Stilton, and I could understand why. The man's presence hampered him and prevented him from giving of his best. I have already explained that the Cheesewright code prohibits brawling if there are females around. The same rule holds good when members of the domestic staff appear at the ringside. If butlers butt in while they are in the process of trying to ascertain the color of some acquaintance's insides, the Cheesewrights cheese it.

But, mark you, they don't like cheesing it, and it is not to be wondered at that, compelled by this major-domo's presence to suspend hostilities, Stilton should have eyed him with ill-concealed animosity. His manner, when he spoke, was brusque.

"What do you want?"

"The door, sir."

Stilton's ill-concealed animosity became rather worse concealed. So packed indeed, with deleterious animal magnetism was the glance he directed at Seppings that one felt that there was a considerable danger of Aunt Dahlia at no distant date finding herself a butler short.

"What do you mean, you want the door? Which door? What door? What on earth do you want a door for?"

I saw that it was almost impossible that he would ever get the thing straight in his mind without a word of explanation, so I supplied it. I always like, if I can, to do the square thing by one and all on these occasions. Scratch Bertram Wooster, I sometimes say, and you find a Boy Scout.

"The front door, Stilton, old dance partner, is what one presumes Pop Seppings has in mind," I said. "I would hazard the guess that the bell rang. Correct, Seppings?"

"Yes, sir," he replied with quiet dignity. "The front door bell rang, and in pursuance of my duties I came to answer it."

And, his manner suggesting that that in his opinion would hold Stilton for awhile, he carried on as planned.

"What I'll bet has happened, Stilton, old scone," I said, clarifying the whole situation, "is that some visitor waits without."

I was right. Seppings flung wide the gates, there was a flash of blonde hair and a whiff of Chanel Number Five, and a girl came sailing in, a girl whom I was able to classify at a single glance as a pipterino of the first water.

Those who know Bertram Wooster best are aware that he is not a man who readily slops over when speaking of the opposite sex. He is cool and critical. He weighs his words. So when I describe this girl as a pipterino, you will gather that she was something pretty special. She could have walked into any assembly of international beauty contestants, and the committee of judges would have laid down the red carpet for her. One could imagine fashionable photographers fighting to the death for her custom.

Like the heroine of *The Mystery of the Pink Crayfish* and, indeed, the heroines of all the thrillers I have ever come across, she had hair the color of ripe wheat and eyes of cornflower blue. Add a tiptilted nose and a figure as full of curves as a scenic railway, and it will not strike you as strange that Stilton, sheathing the sword, should have stood gaping at her dumbly, his aspect that of a man who has been unexpectedly struck by a thunderbolt.

"Is Mrs. Travers around?" inquired this vision, addressing herself to Seppings. "Will you tell her Miss Morehead has arrived."

I was astounded. For some reason, possibly because she had three names, the picture I had formed in my mind of Daphne Dolores Morehead was that of an elderly female with a face like a horse and gold-rimmed pince-nez attached to her top button with a black string. Seeing her steadily and seeing her whole, I found myself commending Aunt Dahlia's sagacity in inviting her to Brinkley Court, presumably to help promote the sale of the *Boudoir*. A word from her, advising its purchase, would, I felt, go a long way with L. G. Trotter. He was doubtless a devoted and excellent husband, true as steel to the wife of his b., but even devoted and excellent husbands are apt to react powerfully when girls of the D. D. Morehead type start giving them Treatment A.

Stilton was still goggling at her like a bulldog confronted with a pound of steak, and now, her eyes of cornflower blue becoming accustomed to the dim light of the hall, she took a dekko at him and uttered an exclamation that seemed—oddly, considering what Stilton was like—one of pleasure.

"Mr. Cheesewright!" she said. "Well, fancy! I thought your face was familiar." She took another dekko. "You *are* D'Arcy Cheesewright, who used to row for Oxford?"

Stilton inclined the bean dumbly. He seemed incapable of speech.

"I thought so. Somebody pointed you out to me at the Eights Week ball one year. But I almost didn't recognize you. You had a moustache then. I'm so glad you haven't any longer. You look so much handsomer without it. I do think moustaches are simply awful. I always say that a man who can lower himself to wearing a moustache might just as well grow a beard."

I could not let this pass.

"There are moustaches and moustaches," I said, twirling mine. Then, seeing that she was asking herself who this slim, distinguished-looking stranger might be, I tapped myself on the wishbone. "Wooster, Bertram," I said. "I'm Mrs. Travers's nephew, she being my aunt. Should I lead you into her presence? She is probably counting the minutes."

She pursed the lips dubiously, as if the program I had suggested deviated in many respects from the ideal.

"Yes, I suppose I ought to be going and saying Hello, but what I would really like would be to explore the grounds. It's such a lovely place."

Stilton, who was now a pretty vermilion, came partially out of the ether, uttering odd, strangled noises like a man with no roof to his mouth trying to recite "Gunga Din." Finally something coherent emerged.

"May I show you round?" he said hoarsely.

"I'd love it."

"Ho!" said Stilton. He spoke quickly, as if feeling he had been remiss in not saying that earlier, and a moment later they were up and doing. And I, with something of the emotions of Daniel passing out of the stage door of the lions' den, went to my room.

It was cool and restful there. Aunt Dahlia is a woman who believes in doing her guests well in the matter of arm chairs and chaise longues, and the chaise longue allotted to me yielded gratefully to the form. It was not long before a pleasant drowsiness stole over me. The weary eyelids closed. I slept.

When I woke up half an hour later, my first act was to start with some violence. The brain cleared by slumber, I had remembered the cosh.

I rose to my feet, appalled, and shot from the room. It was imperative that I should recover possession of that beneficent instrument with all possible speed, for though in our recent encounter I had outgeneraled Stilton in round one, foiling him with my superior footwork and ring science, there was no knowing when he might not be feeling ready for round two. A setback may discourage a Cheesewright for the moment, but does not dispose of him as a logical contender.

The cosh, you will recall, had flashed through the air like a shooting star, to wind up its trip somewhere near Uncle Tom's safe, and I proceeded to the spot on winged feet. And picture my concern on finding on arrival that it wasn't there. The way things disappeared at Brinkley Court . . . ladders, coshes, and what not . . . was enough to make a man throw in his hand and turn his face to the wall.

At this moment I actually did turn my face to the wall, the one the safe was wedged into, and having done so gave another of those violent starts of mine.

And what I saw was enough to make a fellow start with all the violence at his disposal. For two or three ticks I simply couldn't believe it. "Bertram," I said to myself, "the strain has been too much for you. You are cockeyed." But no. I blinked once or twice to clear the vision, and when I had finished blinking there it was, just as I had seen it the first time.

The safe door was open.

18

IT IS AT MOMENTS like this that you catch Bertram Wooster at his superb best, his ice-cold brain working like a machine. Many fellows, I mean to say, seeing that safe door open, would have wasted precious time standing goggling at it, wondering why it was open, who had opened it and why whoever had opened it hadn't shut it again, but not Bertram. Hand him something on a plate with watercress round it, and he does not loiter and linger. He acts. A quick dip inside and a rapid rummaging, and I had the thing all sewed up.

There were half a dozen jewel cases stowed away on the shelves, and it took a minute or two to open them and examine contents, but investigation revealed only one pearl necklace, so I was spared anything in the nature of a perplexing choice. Swiftly trouser-pocketing the *bijouterie*, I shot off to Aunt Dahlia's den like the jack rabbit I had so closely resembled at my recent conference with Stilton. She should, I thought, be there by now, and it was a source of considerable satisfaction to me to feel that I was about to bring the sunshine back into the life of this deserving old geezer. When last seen, she had so plainly been in need of a bit of sunshine.

I found her in statu quo, as foreseen, smoking a gasper and spelling her way through her Agatha Christie, but I didn't bring the sunshine into her life, because it was there already. I was amazed at the change in her demeanor since she had gone off droopingly to see if Uncle Tom had finished talking to Spode about old silver. Then, you will recall, her air had been that of one caught in the machinery. Now, she conveyed the impression of having found the bluebird. As she looked up on discovering me in her midst, her face was shining like the seat of a busdriver's trousers, and it wouldn't have surprised me much if she had started yodeling. Her whole aspect was that of an aunt who on honeydew has fed and drunk the milk of Paradise, and the thought crossed my mind that if she was feeling as yeasty as this before hearing the good news, she might quite easily, when I spilled same, explode with a loud report.

I was not able, however, to reveal the chunk of secret history which I had up my sleeve, for, as so often happens when I am closeted with this woman, she made it impossible for me to get a syllable in edgeways. Even as I crossed the threshold, words began to flutter from her like bats out of a barn.

"Bertie!" she boomed. "Just the boy I wanted to see. Bertie, my pet, I have fought the good fight. Do you remember the hymn about 'See the troops of Midian prowl and prowl around'? It goes on 'Christian, up and smite them,' and that is what I have done in no uncertain manner. Let me tell you what happened. It will make your eyes pop."

"I say," I said, but was able to get no further. She rolled over me like a steam roller.

"When we parted in the hall not long ago, you will

remember, I was bewitched, bothered, and bewildered because I couldn't get hold of Spode to put the bite on him about Eulalie Soeurs, and was going to the collection room on the off chance of there having been a lull. But when I arrived, I found Tom still gassing away, so I took a seat and sat there hoping that Spode would eventually make a break for the open and give me a chance of having a word with him. But he continued to take it without a murmur, and Tom went rambling on. And then suddenly my bones were turned to water and the collection room swam before my eyes. Without any warning Tom suddenly switched to the subject of the necklace. 'You might like to look at it now,' he said. 'Certainly,' said Spode. 'It's in the safe in the hall,' said Tom. 'Let's go,' said Spode, and off they went."

She paused for breath, as even she has to do sometimes.

"I say—" I said.

The lungs refilled, she carried on again.

"I wouldn't have thought my limbs would have been able to support me to the door, much less down a long passage into the hall, but they did. I followed in the wake of the procession, giving at the knees but somehow managing to navigate. What I thought I was doing, joining the party, I don't know, but I suppose I had some vague idea of being present when Tom got the bad news and pleading brokenly for forgiveness. Anyway, I went. Tom opened the safe, and I stood there as if I had been turned into a pillar of salt, like Lot's wife."

I recalled the incident to which she referred, it having happened to come up in the examination paper that time I won that prize for Scripture Knowledge at my private school, but it's probably new to you, so I will give a brief synopsis. For some reason which has escaped my memory they told this Mrs. Lot, while out walking one day, not to look round or she would be turned into a pillar of salt, so of course she immediately did look round and by what I have always thought an odd coincidence she *was* turned into a pillar of salt. It just shows you, what? I mean to say, you never know where you are these days.

"Time marched on. Tom took out the jewel case and passed it over to Spode, who said 'Ah, this is it, is it?' or some damn silly remark like that, and at that moment, with the hand of doom within a toucher of descending, Seppings appeared, probably sent by my guardian angel, and told Tom he was wanted on the phone. 'Eh? What? What?' said Tom, his invariable practice when told he is wanted on the phone, and legged it, followed by Seppings. Woof!" she said, and paused for breath again.

"I say—" I said.

"You can imagine how I felt. That stupendous bit of luck had changed the whole aspect of affairs. For hours I had been wondering how on earth I could get Spode alone, and now I had got him alone. You can bet I didn't waste a second. 'Just think, Lord Sidcup,' I said winningly, 'I haven't had a moment yet to talk to you about all our mutual friends and those happy days at Totleigh Towers. How is dear Sir Watkyn Bassett?' I asked, still winningly. I fairly cooed to the man."

"I say—" I said.

She squelched me with an imperious gesture.

"Don't interrupt, curse you. I never saw such a chap for wanting to collar the conversation. Gabble, gabble, gabble. Listen, can't you, when I'm telling you the biggest story that has broken around these parts for years. Where was I? Oh, yes. 'How is dear Sir Watkyn?' I said, and he said dear Sir Watkyn was pretty oojah-cum-spiff. 'And dear Madeline?' I said, and he said dear Madeline was ticking over all right. And then I drew a deep breath and let him have it. 'And how is that ladies' underclothing place of yours getting along?' I said. 'Eulalie Soeurs, isn't it called? Still coining money, I trust?' And next moment you could have knocked me down with a feather. For with a jolly laugh he replied, 'Eulalie Soeurs? Oh, I haven't anything to do with that any longer. I sold out ages ago. It's a company now.' And as I stood gaping at him, my whole plan of campaign in ruins, he said 'Well, I may as well have a look at this necklace. Mr. Travers says he is anxious to have my opinion of it.' And he pressed his thumb to the catch and the jewel case flew open. And I was just commending my soul to God and saying to myself that this was the end, when I stubbed my foot against something and looked down and there, lying on the floor . . . you'll scarcely believe this . . . was a cosh."

She paused again, took on a cargo of breath quickly, and resumed.

"Yessir, a cosh! You wouldn't know what a cosh is, of course, so I'll explain. It's a small rubber instrument, much used by the criminal classes for socking their friends and relations. They wait till their mother-in-law's back is turned and then let her have it. It's all the rage in underworld circles, and there it was, as I say, lying at my feet."

"I say—" I said.

I got the imperious gesture between the eyes once more.

"Well, for a moment, it rang no bell. I picked it up automatically, the good housewife who doesn't like to see things lying around on floors, but it held no message for me. It simply didn't occur to me that my guardian angel had been directing my footsteps and was showing me the way out of my troubles and perplexities. And then suddenly, in a blinding flash, I got it. I realized what that good old guardian angel was driving at. He had at last succeeded in penetrating the bone and getting it into my fat head. There was Spode, with his back turned, starting to take the necklace out of the case . . ."

I gasped gurglingly.

"You didn't cosh him?"

"Certainly I coshed him. What would you have had me do? What would Napoleon have done? I took a nice easy half-swing and let go with lots of follow-through, and he fell to earth he knew not where."

I could readily believe it. Just so had Constable Dobbs fallen at Deverill Hall.

"He's in bed now, convinced that he had a touch of vertigo and hit his head on the floor. Don't worry about Spode. A good night's rest and a bland diet, and he'll be as right as rain tomorrow. And I've got the necklace, I've got the necklace, I've got the bally necklace, and I feel as if I could pick up a couple of tigers and knock their heads together!"

I gaped at her. The bean was swimming. Through the mist that had risen before the eyes she appeared to be swaying like an aunt caught in a high wind.

"You say you've got the necklace?" I quavered.

"I certainly have."

"Then what," I said, in about as hollow a voice as ever proceeded from human lips, "is this one I've got?"

And I produced my exhibit.

For quite awhile it was plain that she had failed to follow the story sequence. She looked at the necklace, then at me, then at the necklace again. It was not until I had explained fully that she got the strength of it.

"Of course, yes," she said, her brow clearing. "I see it all now. What with yelling for Tom and telling him Spode had had some sort of seizure and listening to him saying 'Oh, my God! Now we'll have to put the frightful fellow up for the night!' and trying to comfort him and helping Seppings tote the remains to bed and all that, I forgot to suggest shutting the safe door. And Tom, of course, never thought of it. He was much too busy tearing his hair and saying this was certainly the last time he would invite a club acquaintance to his house, by golly, it being notorious that the first thing club acquaintances do on finding themselves in somebody's home is to have fits and take advantage of them to stay dug into the woodwork for weeks. And then you came along—"

"—and rummaged in the safe and found a pearl necklace and naturally thought it was yours—"

"—and swiped it. Very decent of you, Bertie dear, and I appreciate the kind thought. If you had been here this morning, I would have told you that Tom insisted on everybody putting their valuables in the safe, but you had dashed up to London. What took you there, by the way?"

"I went to get the cosh, formerly the property of Aunt Agatha's son, Thos. I have been having a little trouble of late with Menaces."

She gazed at me with worshiping eyes, deeply moved.

"Was it you, my heart of gold," she said brokenly, "who provided that cosh? I had been putting it down as straight guardian angel stuff. Oh, Bertie, if ever I called you a brainless poop who ought to be given a scholarship at some good lunatic asylum, I take back the words."

I thanked her briefly.

"But what happens now?"

"I give three rousing cheers and start strewing roses from my hat."

I frowned with a touch of impatience.

"I am not talking about you, my dear old ancestor, but about your nephew Bertram, the latter being waist-high in the mulligatawny and liable at any moment to sink without trace. Here I am in possession of somebody's pearl necklace—"

"Ma Trotter's. I recognize it now. She wears it in the evenings."

"Right. So far, so good. The choker belongs, we find, to Ma Trotter. That point established, what do I do for the best?"

"You put it back."

"In the safe?"

"That's it. You put it back in the safe."

It struck me as a most admirable idea, and I wondered why I hadn't thought of it myself.

"You've hit it!" I said. "Yes, I'll put it back in the safe."

"I'd run along now, if I were you. No time like the present."

"I will. Oh, by the way, Daphne Dolores Morehead has arrived. She's out in the grounds with Stilton."

"What did you think of her?"

"A sight for sore eyes, if I may use the expression. I had no idea they were making female novelists like that these days."

I would have gone on to amplify the favorable impression the young visitor's outer crust had made on me, but at this moment Mrs. Trotter loomed up in the doorway. She looked at me as if feeling that I was on the whole pretty superfluous.

"Oh, good evening, Mr. Wooster," she said in a distant sort of way. "I was hoping to find you alone, Mrs. Travers," she added with the easy tact which had made her the toast of Liverpool.

"I'm just off," I assured her. "Nice evening."

"Very nice."

"Well, toodle-oo," I said, and set a course for the hall, feeling pretty bobbish, for at least a portion of my troubles would soon be over. If, of course, the safe was still open.

It was. And I had reached it and was on the point of whipping out the jewel case and depositing it, when a voice spoke behind me, and turning like a startled fawn, I perceived L. G. Trotter.

Since my arrival at Brinkley Court I had not fraternized to any great extent with this weasel-faced old buster. He gave me the impression, as he had done at that dinner of mine, of not being too frightfully keen on the society of his juniors. I was surprised that he should be wanting to chat with me now, and wished that he could have selected some more suitable moment. With that necklace on my person, solitude was what I desired.

"Hey," he said. "Where's your aunt?"

"She's in her room," I replied, "talking to Mrs. Trotter."

"Oh? Well, when you see her, tell her I've gone to bed." This surprised me.

"To bed? Surely the night is yet young?"

"I've got one of my dyspeptic attacks. You haven't a digestive pill on you?"

"I'm sorry. I came out without any."

"Hell!" he said, rubbing the abdomen. "I'm in agony. I feel as if I'd swallowed a couple of wildcats. Hullo," he proceeded, changing the subject, "what's that safe door doing open?"

I threw out the suggestion that somebody must have opened it, and he nodded as if thinking well of the theory.

"Damned carelessness," he said. "That's the way things get stolen."

And before my bulging eyes he stepped across and gave the door a shove. It closed with a clang.

"Oof!" he said, massaging the abdomen once more, and with a curt "Good night" passed up the stairs, leaving me frozen to the spot. Lot's wife couldn't have been stiffer.

Any chance I had of putting things back in the safe had gone with the wind.

19

I DON'T KNOW that I have a particularly vivid imagination—possibly not, perhaps—but in circs like those which I have just outlined you don't need a very vivid imagination to enable you to spot the shape of things to come. As plainly as if it had been the top line on an oculist's chart, I could see what the future held for Bertram.

As I stood there gaping at that closed door, a vision rose before my eyes, featuring me and an inspector of police, the latter having in his supporting cast an unusually nasty-looking sergeant.

"Are you coming quietly, Wooster?" the inspector was saying.

"Who, me?" I said, quaking in every limb. "I don't know what you mean."

"Ha, ha," laughed the inspector. "That's good. Eh, Fotheringay?"

"Very rich, sir," said the sergeant. "Makes me chuckle, that does."

"Too late to try anything of that sort, my man," went on the inspector, becoming grave again. "The game is up. We have evidence to prove that you went to this safe and from it abstracted a valuable pearl necklace, the property of

Mrs. L. G. Trotter. If that doesn't mean five years in the jug for you, I miss my bet."

"But, honestly, I thought it was Aunt Dahlia's."

"Ha, ha," laughed the inspector.

"Ha, ha," chirped the sergeant.

"A pretty story," said the inspector. "Tell that to the jury and see what they think of it. Fotheringay, the handcuffs!"

Such was the v. that rose before my e. as I gaped at that c.d., and I wilted like a salted snail. Outside in the garden birds were singing their evensong, and it seemed to me that each individual bird was saying "Well, boys, Wooster is for it. We shan't see much of Wooster for the next few years. Too bad, too bad. A nice chap till he took to crime."

A hollow groan escaped my lips, but before another could follow it I was racing for Aunt Dahlia's room. As I reached it, Ma Trotter came out, gave me an austere look and passed on her way, and I went on into the presence. I found the old relative sitting bolt upright in her chair, staring before her with unseeing eyes, and it was plain that once more something had happened to inject a black frost into her sunny mood. The Agatha Christie had fallen unheeded to the floor, displaced from her lap, no doubt, by a shudder of horror.

Normally, I need scarcely say, my policy on finding this sterling old soul looking licked to a splinter would have been to slap her between the shoulder blades and urge her to keep her tail up, but my personal troubles left me with little leisure for bracing aunts. Whatever the disaster or cataclysm that had come upon her, I felt, it could scarcely claim to rank in the same class as the one that had come upon me.

"I say," I said. "The most frightful thing has happened!"

She nodded somberly. A martyr at the stake would have been cheerier.

"You bet your heliotrope socks it has," she responded. "Ma Trotter has thrown off the mask, curse her. She wants Anatole."

"Who wouldn't?"

It seemed for a moment as if she were about to haul off and let a loved nephew have it on the side of the head, but with a strong effort she calmed herself. Well, when I say "calmed herself," she didn't cease to boil briskly, but she confined her activities to the spoken word.

"Don't you understand, ass? She has come out into the open and stated her terms. She says she won't let Trotter buy the *Boudoir* unless I give her Anatole."

It just shows how deeply my predicament had stirred me that my reaction to this frightful speech was practically nil. Informed at any other time that there was even a remote prospect of that superb disher-up handing in his portfolio and going off to waste his sweetness on the desert air of the Trotter home, I should unquestionably have blenched and gasped and tottered but now, as I say, I heard those words virtually unmoved.

"No, really?" I said. "I say, listen, old flesh and blood. Just as I got to the safe and was about to restore the Trotter pearls, that chump L. G. Trotter most officiously shut the door, foiling my aims and objects and leaving me in the dickens of a jam. I'm trembling like a leaf."

"So am I."

"I don't know what to do."

"I don't, either."

"I search in vain for some way out of this what the French call *impasse.*"

"Me, too," she said, picking up the Agatha Christie and

hurling it at a passing vase. When deeply stirred, she is always inclined to kick things and throw things. At Totleigh Towers, during one of our more agitated conferences, she had cleared the mantelpiece in my bedroom of its entire contents, including a terra cotta elephant and a porcelain statuette of the Infant Samuel in Prayer. "I don't suppose any woman ever had such a problem to decide. On the one hand, life without Anatole is a thing almost impossible—"

"Here I am, stuck with this valuable pearl necklace, the property of Mrs. L. G. Trotter, and when its loss—"

"—to contemplate. On the other—"

"—is discovered, hues and cries will be raised, inspectors and sergeants sent for—"

"—hand, I must sell the *Boudoir*, or I can't take that necklace of mine out of hock. So—"

"—and I shall be found with what is known as hot ice on my person."

"Ice!"

"And you know as well as I do what happens to people who are caught in possession of hot ice."

"Ice!" she repeated, and sighed dreamily. "I think of those prawns in iced aspic of his, and I say to myself that I should be mad to face a lifetime without Anatole's cooking. That *Selle d'Agneau à la Grecque!* That *Mignonette de Poulet Rôti Petit Duc!* Those *Nonats de la Méditerranée au Fenouil!* And then I feel I must be practical. I've got to get that necklace back, and if the only way of getting it back is to . . . Sweet suffering soupspoons!" she vociferated, if that's the word, anguish written on her every feature. "I wonder what Tom will say when he hears Anatole is leaving!"

"And I wonder what he'll say when he hears his nephew is doing a stretch in Dartmoor."

"Eh?"

"Stretch in Dartmoor."

"Who's going to do a stretch in Dartmoor?"

"I am."

"You?"

"Me."

"Why?"

I gave her a look which I suppose, strictly speaking, no nephew should have given an aunt. But I was sorely exasperated.

"Haven't you been listening?" I demanded.

She came back at me with equal heat.

"Of course I haven't been listening. Do you think that when I am faced with the prospect of losing the finest cook in the midland counties I have time to pay attention to your vapid conversation? What were you babbling about?"

I drew myself up. The word "babbling" had wounded me.

"I was merely mentioning that, owing to that ass L. G. Trotter having shut the door of the safe before I could deposit the fatal necklace, I am landed with the thing. I described it as hot ice."

"Oh, that was what you were saying about ice?"

"That was what. I also hazarded the prediction that in about two shakes of a duck's tail inspectors and sergeants would come scooping me up and taking me off to chokey."

"What nonsense. Why should anyone think you had anything to do with it?"

I laughed. One of those short, bitter ones.

"You don't think it may arouse their suspicions when they find the ruddy thing in my trouser pocket? At any moment I may be caught with the goods on me, and you don't have to read many thrillers to know what happens to unfortunate slobs who are caught with the goods on them. They get it in the neck."

I could see she was profoundly moved. In my hours of ease this aunt is sometimes uncertain, coy and hard to please and, when I was younger, not infrequently sloshed me on the earhole if my behavior seemed to her to call for the gesture, but let real peril threaten Bertram and she is in there swinging every time.

"This isn't good," she said, picking up a small foot-stool and throwing it at a china shepherdess on the mantel-piece.

I endorsed this view, expressing the opinion that it was dashed awful.

"You'll have to—"

"Hist!"

"Eh?"

"Hist!"

"What do you mean, Hist?"

What I had meant by the monosyllable was that I had heard footsteps approaching the door. Before I could explain this, the handle turned sharply and Uncle Tom came in.

My ear told me at once that all was not well with this relative by marriage. When Uncle Tom has anything on his mind, he rattles his keys. He was jingling now like a xylophone. His face had the haggard, careworn look which it wears when he hears that week-end guests are expected.

"It's a judgment!" he said, bursting into speech with a whoosh.

Aunt Dahlia masked her agitation with what I imagine she thought to be a genial smile.

"Hullo, Tom, come and join the party. What's a judgment?"

"This is. On me. For weakly allowing you to invite those infernal Trotters here. I knew something awful would happen. I felt it in my bones. You can't fill the house up with people like that without courting disaster. Stands to reason. He's got a face like a weasel, she's twenty pounds overweight, and that son of hers wears whiskers. It was madness ever to let them cross the threshold. Do you know what's happened?"

"No, what?"

"Somebody's pinched her necklace!"

"Good heavens!"

"I thought that would make you sit up," said Uncle Tom, with gloomy triumph. "She collared me in the hall just now and said she wanted the thing to wear at dinner tonight, and I took her to the safe and opened it and it wasn't there."

I told myself that I must keep very cool.

"You mean," I said, "that it had gone?"

He gave me rather an unpleasant look.

"You've got a lightning brain!" he said.

Well, I have, of course.

"But how could it have gone?" I asked. "Was the safe open?"

"No, shut. But I must have left it open. All that fuss of putting that frightful fellow Sidcup to bed distracted my attention."

I think he was about to say that it just showed what happened when you let people like that into the house, but checked himself on remembering that he was the one who had invited him.

"Well, there it is," he said. "Somebody seems to have

come along while we were upstairs, seen the safe door open and helped himself. The Trotter woman is raising cain, and it was only my urgent entreaties that kept her from sending for the police there and then. I told her we could get much better results by making secret inquiries. Didn't want a scandal, I said. But I doubt if I could have persuaded her if it hadn't been that young Gorringe came along and backed me up. Quite an intelligent young fellow, that, though he does wear whiskers."

I cleared my throat nonchalantly. At least, I tried to do it nonchalantly.

"Then what steps are you taking, Uncle Tom?"

"I'm going to excuse myself during dinner on the plea of a headache—which I've got, I don't mind telling you—and go and search the rooms. Just possible I might dig up something. Meanwhile, I'm off to get a drink. The whole thing has upset me considerably. Will you join me in a quick one, Bertie, me boy?"

"I think I'll stick on here, if you don't mind," I said. "Aunt Dahlia and I are talking of this and that."

He produced a final obligato on the keys.

"Well, suit yourself. But it seems odd to me in my present frame of mind that anyone can refuse a drink. I wouldn't have thought it possible."

As the door closed behind him, Aunt Dahlia expelled her breath like a death rattle.

"Golly!" she said.

It seemed to me the *mot juste*.

"What should we do now, do you think?" I queried.

"I know what I'd like to do. I'd like to put the whole thing up to Jeeves, if certain fatheads hadn't let him go off on toots in London just when we need him most."

"He may be back by now."

"Ring for Seppings, and ask."

I pressed the bell.

"Oh, Seppings," I said, as he entered and You-rang-madam-ed. "Has Jeeves got back yet?"

"Yes, sir."

"Then send him here with all speed," I said.

And a few moments later the man was with us, looking so brainy and intelligent that my heart leaped up as if I had beheld a rainbow in the sky.

"Oh, Jeeves," I yipped.

"Oh, Jeeves," yipped Aunt Dahlia, dead heating with me.

"After you," I said.

"No, go ahead," she replied, courteously yielding the floor. "Your predicament is worse than my predicament. Mine can wait."

I was touched.

"Very handsome of you, old egg," I said. "Much appreciated. Jeeves, your close attention, if you please. Certain problems have arisen."

"Yes, sir?"

"Two in all."

"Yes, sir?"

"Shall we call them Problem A. and Problem B.?"

"Certainly, sir, if you wish."

"Then here is Problem A., the one affecting me."

I ran through the scenario, putting the facts clearly and well.

"So there you are, Jeeves. Bend the brain to it. If you wish to pace the corridor, by all means do so."

"It will not be necessary, sir. One sees what must be done."

I said I would be glad if he could arrange it so that two could.

"You must restore the necklace to Mrs. Trotter, sir."

"Give it back to her, you mean?"

"Precisely, sir."

"But, Jeeves," I said, my voice shaking a little, "isn't she going to wonder how I come to have my hooks on the thing? Will she not probe and question, and having probed and questioned rush to the telephone and put in her order for inspectors and sergeants?"

A muscle at the side of his mouth twitched indulgently.

"The restoration would, of course, have to be accomplished with secrecy, sir. I would advocate placing the piece of jewelry in the lady's bedchamber at a moment when it was unoccupied. Possibly while she was at the dinner table."

"But I should be at the dinner table, too. I can't say 'Oh, excuse me' and dash upstairs in the middle of the fish course."

"I was about to suggest that you allow me to attend to the matter, sir. My movements will be less circumscribed."

"You mean you'll handle the whole binge?"

"If you will give me the piece of jewelry, sir, I shall be most happy to do so."

I was overcome. I burned with remorse and shame. I saw how mistaken I had been in supposing that he had been talking through the back of his neck.

"Golly, Jeeves! This is a pretty feudal."

"Not at all, sir."

"You've solved the whole thing. Rem . . . what's that expression of yours?"

"*Rem acu tetigisti,* sir?"

"That's it. It does mean 'You have put your finger on the nub,' doesn't it?"

"That would be a rough translation of the Latin, sir. I am happy to have given satisfaction. But did I understand you to say that there was a further matter that was troubling you, sir?"

"Problem B. is mine, Jeeves," said Aunt Dahlia, who during this slice of dialogue had been waiting in the wings, chafing a bit at being withheld from taking the stage. "It's about Anatole."

"Yes, madam?"

"Mrs. Trotter wants him."

"Indeed, madam?"

"And she says she won't let Trotter buy the *Boudoir* unless she gets him. And you know how vital it is that I sell the *Boudoir*. Sweet spirits of niter!" cried the old relative passionately. "If only there was some way of inserting a bit of backbone into L. G. Trotter and making him stand up to the woman and defy her!"

"There is, madam."

Aunt Dahlia leaped about a foot and a quarter. It was as though that calm response had been a dagger of Oriental design thrust into the fleshy part of her leg.

"What did you say, Jeeves? Did you say there was?"

"Yes, madam. I think it will be a reasonably simple matter to induce Mr. Trotter to override the lady's wishes."

I didn't want to cast a damper over the proceedings, but I had to put in a word here.

"Frightfully sorry to have to dash the cup of joy from your lips, old tortured spirit," I said, "but I fear that all this comes under the head of wishful thinking. Pull yourself together, Jeeves. You speak . . . is it airily?"

"Airily or glibly, sir."

"Thank you, Jeeves. You speak airily or glibly of inducing L. G. Trotter to throw off the yoke and defy his considerably better half, but are you not too . . . dash it, I've forgotten the word."

"Sanguine, sir?"

"That's it. Sanguine. Brief though my acquaintance with these twain has been, I have got L. G. Trotter's number, all right. His attitude towards Ma Trotter is that of an exceptionally diffident worm towards a sinewy Plymouth Rock or Orpington. A word from her, and he curls up into a ball. So where do you get off with that simple-matter-to-override-wishes stuff?"

I thought I had him there, but no.

"If I might explain. I gather from Mr. Seppings, who has had opportunities of overhearing the lady's conversation, that Mrs. Trotter, being socially ambitious, is extremely anxious to see Mr. Trotter knighted, madam."

Aunt Dahlia nodded.

"Yes, that's right. She's always talking about it. She thinks it would be one in the eyes for Mrs. Alderman Blenkinsop."

"Precisely, madam."

I was rather surprised.

"Do they knight birds like him?"

"Oh, yes, sir. A gentleman of Mr. Trotter's prominence in the world of publishing is always in imminent danger of receiving the accolade."

"Danger? Don't these bozos like being knighted?"

"Not when they are of Mr. Trotter's retiring disposition, sir. He would find it a very testing ordeal. It involves wearing satin knee-breeches and walking backwards with a sword between the legs, not at all the sort of thing a sensitive gentleman of regular habits would enjoy. And he shrinks, no doubt, from the prospect of being addressed for the remainder of his life as Sir Lemuel."

"His name's not Lemuel?"

"I fear so, sir."

"Couldn't he use his second name?"

"His second name is Gengulphus."

"Golly, Jeeves," I said, thinking of old Uncle Tom Portarlington, "there's some raw work pulled at the font from time to time, is there not?"

"There is, indeed, sir."

Aunt Dahlia seemed perplexed, like one who strives in vain to put her finger on the nub.

"Is this all leading up to something, Jeeves?"

"Yes, madam. I was about to hazard the suggestion that were Mr. Trotter to become aware that the alternative to buying *Milady's Boudoir* was the discovery by Mrs. Trotter that he had been offered a knighthood and had declined it, you might find the gentleman more easily molded than in the past, madam."

It took Aunt Dahlia right between the eyes like a sock full of wet sand. She tottered, and grabbed for support at the upper part of my right arm, giving it the dickens of a pinch. The anguish caused her next remark to escape me, though as it was no doubt merely "Gosh!" or "Lord love a duck!" or something of that sort, I suppose I didn't miss much. When the mists had cleared from my eyes and I was myself again, Jeeves was speaking.

"It appears that Mrs. Trotter some months ago insisted on Mr. Trotter engaging the services of a gentleman's personal gentleman, a young fellow named Worple, and Worple contrived to secure the rough draft of Mr. Trotter's letter of refusal from the wastepaper basket. He had recently become a member of the Junior Ganymede, and in accordance with Rule Eleven he forwarded the document to the secretary for inclusion in the club archives.

Through the courtesy of the secretary I was enabled to peruse it after luncheon, and a photostatic copy is to be dispatched to me through the medium of the post. I think that if you were to mention this to Mr. Trotter, madam—"

Aunt Dahlia uttered a whoop similar in timbre to those which she had been accustomed to emit in the old Quorn and Pytchley days when encouraging a bevy of hounds to get on the scent and give it both nostrils.

"We've got him cold!"

"So one is disposed to imagine, madam."

"I'll tackle him right away."

"You can't," I pointed out. "He's gone to bed. Touch of dyspepsia."

"Then tomorrow directly after breakfast," said Aunt Dahlia. "Oh, Jeeves!"

Emotion overcame her, and she grabbed at my arm again. It was like being bitten by an alligator.

20

AT ABOUT THE hour of nine next morning a singular spectacle might have been observed on the main staircase of Brinkley Court. It was Bertram Wooster coming down to breakfast.

It is a fact well known to my circle that only on very rare occasions do I squash in at the communal morning meal, preferring to chew the kipper or whatever it may be in the seclusion of my bedchamber. But a determined man can nerve himself to almost anything, if necessary, and I was resolved at all cost not to miss the dramatic moment when Aunt Dahlia tore off her whiskers and told a cowering L. G. Trotter that she knew all. It would, I felt, be value for money.

Though slightly on the somnambulistic side, I don't know when I have felt more strongly that the lark was on the wing and the snail on the thorn and God in His Heaven and all right with the world. Thanks to Jeeves's outstanding acumen, Aunt Dahlia's problems were solved, and I was in a position—if I cared to be rude enough—to laugh in the faces of any inspectors and sergeants who might blow in. Furthermore, before retiring to rest on the previous night I had taken the precaution to recover the cosh from the old relative, and it was securely on my person once more. Little wonder that, as I entered the dining-room, I was within an ace of bursting into song and piping as the linnets do, as I have heard Jeeves put it.

The first thing I saw on crossing the threshold was Stilton wolfing ham, the next Daphne Dolores Morehead finishing off her repast with toast and marmalade.

"Ah, Bertie, old man," cried the former, waving a fork in the friendliest manner. "So there you are, Bertie, old fellow. Come in, Bertie, old chap, come in. Splendid to see you looking so rosy."

His cordiality would have surprised me more, if I hadn't seen in it a ruse or stratagem designed to put me off my guard and lull me into a false sense of security. Keenly alert, I went to the sideboard and helped myself with my left hand to sausages and bacon, keeping the right hand on the cosh in my side pocket. This jungle warfare teaches a man to take no chances.

"Nice morning," I said, having taken my seat and dipped the lips into a cup of coffee.

"Lovely," agreed the Morehead, who was looking more than ever like a dewy flower at daybreak. "D'Arcy is going to take me for a row on the river."

"Yes," said Stilton, giving her a burning glance. "One feels that Daphne ought to see the river. You might tell your aunt we shall not be back for lunch. Sandwiches and hardboiled eggs are being provided."

"By that nice butler."

"By, as you say, that nice butler, who also thought it might run to a bottle of the best from the oldest bin. We shall be starting almost immediately."

"I'll be going and getting ready," said the Morehead.

She rose with a bright smile, and Stilton, full though he

was of ham, bounded gallantly to open the door for her. When he returned to the table, he found me rather ostentatiously brandishing the cosh. It seemed to surprise him.

"Hullo!" he said. "What are you doing with that thing?"

"Oh, nothing," I replied nonchalantly, resting it by my plate. "I just thought I would like to have it handy."

He swallowed a chunk of ham in a puzzled way. Then his face cleared.

"Good Lord! You didn't think I was going to set about you?"

I said that some such idea had crossed my mind, and he uttered an amused laugh.

"Good heavens, no. Why, I look on you as my dearest pal, old man."

It seemed to me that if yesterday's session was a specimen of the way he comported himself towards his dearest pals, the ones who weren't quite so dear must have a pretty thin time of it. I said as much, and he laughed again as heartily as if he had been standing in the dock at Vinton Street police court with His Worship getting off those nifties of his which convulsed all and sundry.

"Oh, that?" he said, dismissing the incident with an airy wave of the hand. "Forget all that, dear old chap. Put it right out of your mind. Perhaps I was a little cross on the occasion to which you refer, but no longer."

"No?" I said guardedly.

"Definitely not. I see now that I owe you a deep debt of gratitude. But for you, I might still be engaged to that pill Florence. Thank you, Bertie, old man."

Well, I said "Not at all" or "Don't mention it" or something of that sort, but my head was swimming. What with getting up for breakfast and hearing this Cheesewright allude to Florence as a pill, I felt in a sort of dream.

"I thought you loved her," I said, digging a bewildered fork into my sausage.

He laughed again. Only a beefy mass of heartiness like G. D'Arcy Cheesewright could have been capable of so much merriment at such an hour.

"Who, me? Good heavens, no. I may have imagined I did once . . . one of those boyish fancies . . . but when she said I had a head like a pumpkin, the scales fell from my eyes and I came out of the ether. Pumpkin, forsooth! I don't mind telling you, Bertie, old chap, that there are others—I mention no names—who have described my head as majestic. Yes, I have it from a reliable source that it makes me look a king among men. That will give you a rough idea of what a silly young geezer that blighted Florence Craye is. It is a profound relief to me that you have enabled me to get her out of my hair."

He thanked me again, and I said "Don't mention it," or it may have been "Not at all." I was feeling dizzier than ever.

"Then you don't think," I said with a quaver in the v., "that later on, when the hot blood has cooled, there might be a reconciliation?"

"Not a hope."

"It happened before."

"It won't happen again. I know now what love really is, Bertie. I tell you, when somebody—who shall be nameless—gazes into my eyes and says that the first time she saw me—in spite of the fact that I was wearing a moustache fully as foul as that one of yours—something went over her like an electric shock, I feel as if I had just won the Diamond Sculls at Henley. It's all washed up between Florence and me. She's yours, old man. Take her, old chap, take her."

Well, I said something civil like "Oh, thanks," but he wasn't listening. A silvery voice had called his name, and pausing but an instant to swallow the last of his ham he shot from the room, his face aglow and his eyes a-sparkle.

He left me with the heart like lead within the bosom and the sausage and bacon turning to ashes in my mouth. This, I could see, was the end. It was plain to the least observant eye that G. D'Arcy Cheesewright had got it properly up his nose. Morehead Preferred was booming, and Craye Ordinaries down in the cellar with no takers.

And I had been so certain that in due season wiser counsels would prevail, causing these two sundered hearts to regret the rift in the lute and decide to have another pop at it, thus saving me from the scaffold once more. But it was not to be. Bertram was for it. He would have to drain the bitter cup, after all.

I was starting on a second installment of coffee—it tasted like the bitter cup—when L. G. Trotter came in.

The one thing I didn't want in my enfeebled state was to have to chew the fat with Trotters, but when you're alone in a dining-room with a fellow, something in the nature of conversation is inevitable, so, as he poured himself out a cup of tea, I said it was a beautiful morning and recommended the sausages and bacon.

He reacted strongly, shuddering from head to foot.

"Sausages?" he said. "Bacon?" he said. "Don't talk to me about sausages and bacon," he said. "My dyspepsia's worse than ever."

Well, if he wanted to thresh out the subject of his aching tum, I was prepared to lend a ready ear, but he skipped on to another topic.

"You married?" he asked.

I winced a trifle and said I wasn't actually married yet.

"And you won't ever be, if you've got a morsel of sense," he proceeded, and brooded darkly over his tea for a moment. "You know what happens when you get married? You're bossed. You can't call your soul your own. You become just a cipher in the home."

I must say I was a bit surprised to find him so confidential to one who was, after all, a fairly mere stranger, but I put it down to the dyspepsia. No doubt the shooting pains had robbed him of his cool judgment.

"Have an egg," I said, by way of showing him that my heart was in the right place.

He turned green and tied himself into a lovers' knot.

"I won't have an egg! Don't keep telling me to have things. Do you think I could look at eggs, feeling the way I do? It's all this infernal French cooking. No digestion can stand up against it. Marriage!" he said, getting back to the old subject. "Don't talk to me about marriage. You get married, and first thing you know, you have stepsons rung in on you who grow whiskers and don't do a stroke of honest work. All they do is write poems about sunsets. Pah!"

I'm pretty shrewd, and it flashed upon me at this point that it might quite possibly be his stepson Percy to whom he was guardedly alluding. But before I could verify this suspicion the room had begun to fill up. Round about nine-twenty, which it was now, you generally find the personnel of a country house lining up for the eats. Aunt Dahlia came in and took a fried egg. Mrs. Trotter came in and took a sausage. Percy and Florence came in and took respectively a slice of ham and a portion of haddock. As there were no signs of Uncle Tom, I presumed that he was breakfasting in bed. He generally does, rarely feeling equal to facing his guests till he has fortified himself a bit for the stern ordeal.

Those present had got their heads down and their elbows squared and were busily employed getting theirs, when Seppings appeared with the morning papers, and conversation, not that there had ever been much of it, flagged. It was to a silent gathering that there now entered a newcomer, a man about seven feet in height with a square, powerful face, slightly moustached toward the center. It was some time since I had set eyes on Roderick Spode, but I had no difficulty in recognizing him. He was one of those distinctive-looking blisters who, once seen, are never forgotten.

He was looking a little paler, I thought, as if he had recently had an attack of vertigo and hit his head on the floor. He said "Good morning" in what for him was rather a weak voice, and Aunt Dahlia glanced up from her *Daily Mirror*.

"Why, Lord Sidcup!" she said. "I never expected that you would be able to come to breakfast. Are you sure it's wise? Do you feel better this morning?"

"Considerably better, thank you," he responded bravely. "The swelling has to some extent subsided."

"I'm so glad. That's those cold compresses. I was hoping they would bring home the bacon. Lord Sidcup," said Aunt Dahlia, "had a nasty fall yesterday evening. We think it must have been a sudden giddiness. Everything went black, didn't it, Lord Sidcup?"

He nodded, and was plainly sorry next moment that he had done so, for he winced as I have sometimes winced when rashly oscillating the bean after some outstanding night of revelry at the Drones.

"Yes," he said. "It was all most extraordinary. I was standing there feeling perfectly well—never better, in fact—when it was as though something hard had hit me on the head, and I remembered no more till I came to in my room, with you smoothing my pillow and your butler mixing me a cooling drink."

"That's life," said Aunt Dahlia gravely. "Yessir, that's life all right. Here today and gone tomorrow, I often say. Bertie, you hellhound, take that beastly cigarette of yours outside. It smells like guano."

I rose, always willing to oblige, and had sauntered about halfway to the french window, when from the lips of Mrs. L. G. Trotter there suddenly proceeded what I can only describe as a screech. I don't know if you have ever inadvertently trodden on an unseen cat. Much the same sort of thing. Taking a quick look at her, I saw that her face had become almost as red as Aunt Dahlia's.

"Well!" she ejaculated.

She was staring at the *Times*, which was what she had drawn in the distribution of the morning journals, in much the same manner as a resident of India would have stared at a cobra, had he found it nestling in his bath tub.

"Of all the—!" she said, and then words failed her.

L. G. Trotter gave her the sort of look the cobra might have given the resident of India who had barged in on its morning bath. I could understand how he felt. A man with dyspepsia, already out of harmony with his wife, does not like to hear that wife screaming her head off in the middle of breakfast.

"What on earth's the matter?" he said testily.

Her bosom heaved like a stage sea.

"I'll tell you what's the matter. They've gone and knighted Robert Blenkinsop!"

"They have?" said L. G. Trotter. "Gosh!"

The stricken woman seemed to think "Gosh!" inadequate.

"Is that all you can say?"

It wasn't. He now said "Ba goom!" She continued to erupt like one of those volcanoes which spill over from time to time and make the neighboring householders think a bit.

"Robert Blenkinsop! Robert Blenkinsop! Of all the iniquitous pieces of idiocy! I don't know what things are coming to nowadays. I never heard of such a . . . May I ask why you are laughing?"

L. G. Trotter curled up beneath her eye like a sheet of carbon paper.

"Not laughing," he said meekly. "Just smiling. I was thinking of Bobby Blenkinsop walking backwards with satin knee-breeches on."

"Oh?" said Ma Trotter, and her voice rang through the room like that of a costermonger indicating to his public that he has Brussels sprouts and blood oranges for sale. "Well, let me tell you that that is never going to happen to you. If ever you are offered a knighthood, Lemuel, you will refuse it. Do you understand? I won't have you cheapening yourself."

There was a crash. It was Aunt Dahlia dropping her coffee cup, and I could appreciate her emotion. She was feeling precisely as I had felt on learning from Percy that the Wooster Darts sweep ticket had changed hands, leaving Stilton free to attack me with tooth and claw. There is nothing that makes a woman sicker than the sudden realization that somebody she thought she was holding in the hollow of her hand isn't in the hollow of her hand by a jugful. So far from being in the hollow of her hand, L. G. Trotter was stepping high, wide and handsome with his hat on the side of his head, and I wasn't surprised that the thing had shaken her to her foundation garments.

In the silence which followed L. G. Trotter's response to this wifely ultimatum—it was, if I remember correctly, "Okay"—Seppings appeared in the doorway.

He was carrying a silver salver, and on this salver lay a pearl necklace.

21

It is pretty generally recognized in the circles in which he moves that Bertram Wooster is not a man who lightly throws in the towel and admits defeat. Beneath the thingummies of what-d'you-call-it his head, wind, and weather permitting, is as a rule bloody but unbowed, and if the slings and arrows of outrageous fortune want to crush his proud spirit, they have to pull their socks up and make a special effort.

Nevertheless, I must confess that when, already weakened by having come down to breakfast, I beheld the spectacle which I have described, I definitely quailed. The heart sank, beads of persp. sprang out upon the brow and, as had happened in the case of Spode, everything went black. Through a murky mist I seemed to be watching a Negro butler presenting an inky salver to a Ma Trotter who looked like the end man in a minstrel show.

The floor heaved beneath my feet as if an earthquake had set in with unusual severity. My eye, in a fine frenzy rolling, met Aunt Dahlia's, and I saw that hers was rolling, too.

Still, she did her best, as always.

"'At-a-boy, Seppings!" she said heartily. "We were all

wondering where that necklace could have got to. It is yours, isn't it, Mrs. Trotter?"

Ma Trotter was scrutinizing the salver through a lorgnette.

"It's mine, all right," she said. "But what I'd like to know is how it came into this man's possession."

Aunt Dahlia continued to do her best.

"You found it on the floor of the hall, I suppose, Seppings, where Lord Sidcup dropped it when he had his seizure?"

A dashed good suggestion, I thought, and it might quite easily have clicked, had not Spode, the silly ass, shoved his oar in.

"I fail to see how that could be so, Mrs. Travers," he said in that supercilious way of his which has got him so disliked on all sides. "The necklace I was holding when my senses left me was yours. Mrs. Trotter's was presumably in the safe."

"Yes," said Ma Trotter, "and pearl necklaces don't jump out of safes. I think I'll step to the telephone and have a word with the police."

Aunt Dahlia raised her eyebrows. It must have taken a bit of doing, but she did it.

"I don't understand you, Mrs. Trotter," she said, very much the *grande dame*. "Do you suppose that my butler would break into the safe and steal your necklace?"

Spode horned in again. He was one of those unpleasant men who never know when to keep their big mouths shut.

"Why break?" he said. "It would not have been necessary to *break* into the safe. The door was already open."

"Ho!" cried Ma Trotter, reckless of the fact that the copyright of the word was Stilton's. "So that's how it was.

All he had to do was reach in and help himself. The telephone is in the hall, I think?"

Seppings made his first contribution to the feast of reason and flow of soul.

"If I might explain, madam."

He spoke austerely. The rules of their guild do not permit butlers to give employers' guests dirty looks, but while stopping short of the dirty look he was not affectionate. Her loose talk about police and telephones had caused him to take umbrage, and it was pretty clear that whoever he might select as a companion on his next long walking tour, it would not be Ma Trotter.

"It was not I who found the necklace, madam. Acting upon instructions from Mr. Travers, I instituted a search through the rooms of the staff and discovered the object in the bedchamber of Mr. Wooster's personal attendant, Mr. Jeeves. Upon my drawing this to Mr. Jeeves's attention, he informed me that he had picked it up in the hall."

"Is that so? Well, tell this man Jeeves to come here at once."

"Very good, madam."

Seppings withdrew, and I would have given a good deal to have been able to withdraw myself, for in about another two ticks, I saw, it would be necessary for Bertram Wooster to come clean and reveal all, blazoning forth to the world Aunt Dahlia's recent activities, if blazoning forth to the world is the expression I want, and bathing the unfortunate old egg in shame and confusion. Feudal fidelity would no doubt make Jeeves seal his lips, but you can't let fellows go sealing their lips if it means rendering themselves liable to an exemplary sentence, coupled with some strong remarks from the Bench. Come what might, the dirt would have to be dished. The code of the Woosters is rigid on points like this.

Looking at Aunt Dahlia, I could see that her mind was working along the same lines, and she wasn't liking it by any means. With a face as red as hers she couldn't turn pale, but her lips were tightly set and her hand, as it lathered a slice of toast with marmalade, plainly shook. The look on her dial was the look of a woman who didn't need a fortune teller and a crystal ball to apprise her of the fact that it would not be long before the balloon went up.

I was gazing at her so intently that it was only when a soft cough broke the silence that I realized that Jeeves had joined the gang. He was standing on the outskirts looking quietly respectful.

"Madam?" he said.

"Hey, you!" said Ma Trotter.

He continued to look quietly respectful. If he resented having the words "Hey, you!" addressed to him, there was nothing in his manner to show it.

"This necklace," said Ma Trotter, giving him a double whammy through the lorgnette. "The butler says he found it in your room."

"Yes, madam. I was planning after breakfast to make inquiries as to its ownership."

"You were, were you?"

"I presumed that it was some trinket belonging to one of the housemaids."

"It was . . . *what?*"

He coughed again, that deferential cough of his which sounds like a well-bred sheep clearing its throat on a distant mountain top.

"I perceived at once that it was merely an inexpensive imitation made from cultured pearls, madam," he said.

I don't know if you happen to know the expression "a stunned silence." I've come across it in books when one of the characters has unloaded a hot one on the assembled company, and I have always thought it a neat way of describing that sort of stilly hush that pops up on these occasions. The silence that fell on the Brinkley Court breakfast table as Jeeves uttered these words was as stunned as the dickens.

L. G. Trotter was the first to break it.

"What's that? Inexpensive imitation? I paid five thousand pounds for that necklace."

"Of course you did," said Ma Trotter with a petulant waggle of the bean. "The man's intoxicated."

I felt compelled to intervene in the debate and dispel the miasma of suspicion which had arisen, or whatever it is that miasmas do.

"Intoxicated?" I said. "At ten in the morning? A laughable theory. But the matter can readily be put to the test. Jeeves, say 'Theodore Oswaldtwistle, the thistle sifter, in sifting a sack of thistles thrust three thorns through the thick of his thumb.'"

He did so with an intonation as clear as a bell, if not clearer.

"You see," I said, and rested my case.

Aunt Dahlia, who had blossomed like a flower revived with a couple of fluid ounces of the right stuff from a watering can, chipped in with a helpful word.

"You can bank on Jeeves," she said, "If he thinks it's a dud, it is a dud. He knows all about jewelry."

"Precisely," I added. "He has the full facts. He studied under an aunt of his in the profession."

"Cousin, sir."

"Of course, yes, cousin. Sorry, Jeeves."

"Not at all, sir."

Spode came butting in again.

"Let me see that necklace," he said authoritatively.

Jeeves drew the salver to his attention.

"You will, I think, support my view, my lord."

Spode took contents, glanced at them, sniffed and delivered judgment.

"Perfectly correct. An imitation, and not a very good one."

"You can't be sure," said Percy, and got withered by a look.

"Can't be sure?" Spode bristled like a hornet whose feelings have been wounded by a tactless remark. "Can't be *sure*?"

"Of course he's sure," I said, not actually slapping him on the back but giving him a back-slapping look designed to show him he had got Bertram Wooster in his corner. "He knows, as everybody knows, that cultured pearls have a core. You spotted the core in a second, didn't you, Spode, old man, or rather Lord Sidcup, old man?"

I was going on to speak of the practice of introducing a foreign substance into the oyster in order to kid it along and induce it to cover this f.s. with layers of nacre—which I still think is a dirty trick to play on a shellfish which simply wants to be left alone with its thoughts—but Spode had risen. There was dudgeon in his manner.

"All this sort of thing at breakfast!" he said, and I saw what he meant. At home, no doubt, he wrapped himself around the morning egg in cozy seclusion, his daily paper propped up against the coffee pot and none of this business of naked passions buzzing all over the place. He wiped his mouth, and left via the french window, wincing with a hand to his head as L. G. Trotter spoke in a voice that nearly cracked his tea cup.

"Emily! Explain this!"

Ma Trotter got the lorgnette working on him, but for all the good it did she might as well have used a monocle. He stared right back at her, and I imagine—couldn't be certain, of course, because his back was to me—that there was in his gaze a steely hardness that turned her bones to water. At any rate, when she spoke, it was like what I have heard Jeeves describe as the earliest pipe of half-awakened birds.

"I can't explain it," she . . . yes, quavered. I was going to say "murmured," but quavered hits it off better.

L. G. Trotter barked like a seal.

"I can," he said. "You've been giving money on the sly again to that brother of yours."

This was the first I had heard of any brother of Ma Trotter's, but I wasn't surprised. My experience is that all wives of prosperous businessmen have shady brothers in the background to whom they slip a bit from time to time.

"I haven't!"

"Don't lie to me!"

"Oh!" cried the shrinking woman, shrinking a bit more, and the spectacle was too much for Percy. All this while he had been sitting tensely where he sat, giving the impression of something stuffed by a good taxidermist, but now, moved by a mother's distress, he rose rather in the manner of one about to reply to the toast of The Ladies. He was looking a little like a cat in a strange alley which is momentarily expecting a half brick in the short ribs, but his voice, though low, was firm.

"I can explain everything. Moth-aw is innocent. She wanted her necklace cleaned. She entrusted it to me to take to the jeweler's, and I pawned it and had an imitation made. I needed money urgently."

Aunt Dahlia well-I'll-be-blowed.

"What an extraordinary thing to do!" she said. "Did you ever hear of anybody doing anything like that, Bertie?"

"New to me, I must confess."

"Amazing, eh?"

"Bizarre, you might call it."

"Still, that's how it goes."

"Yes, that's how it goes."

"I needed a thousand pounds to put into the play," said Percy.

L. G. Trotter, who was in good voice this morning, uttered a howl that set the silverware rattling. It was fortunate for Spode that he had removed himself from earshot, for it would certainly have done that head of his no good. Even I, though a strong man, leaped about six inches.

"You put a thousand pounds into a *play*?"

"Into *the* play," said Percy. "Florence's and mine. My dramatization of her novel, *Spindrift*. One of our backers had failed us, and rather than disappoint the woman I loved—"

Florence was staring at him, wide-eyed. If you remember, I described her aspect on first glimpsing my moustache as having had in it a touch of the Soul's Awakening. The S.A. was now even more pronounced. It stuck out a mile.

"Percy! You did that for me?"

"And I'd do it again," said Percy.

L. G. Trotter began to speak. As to whether he opened his remarks with the words "Ba goom!" I cannot be positive, but there was a "Ba goom!" implicit in every syllable. The man had got it right up his nose, and one felt a gentle pity for Ma Trotter, little as one liked her. Her reign was over. She had had it. From now on it was plain who was going to be the Führer of the Trotter home. The worm of yesterday—or you might say the worm of ten minutes ago—had become a worm in tiger's clothing.

"This settles it!" he vociferated, if vociferated is the word. "There won't be any more loafing about London for you, young man. We leave this house this morning—"

"What!" yipped Aunt Dahlia.

"—and the moment we get back to Liverpool you start in at the bottom of the business, as you ought to have done two years ago if I hadn't let myself be persuaded against my better judgment. Five thousand pounds I paid for that necklace, and you . . ."

Emotion overcame him, and he paused.

"But, Mr. Trotter!" There was anguish in Aunt Dahlia's voice. "You aren't leaving this morning!"

"Yes, I am. Think I'm going to go through another of that French cook's lunches?"

"But I was hoping you would not be going away before we had settled this matter of buying the *Boudoir*. If you could give me a few moments in the library?"

"No time for that. I'm going to drive in to Market Snodsbury and see a doctor. Just a chance he may be able to do something to relieve the pain. It's about here that it seems to catch me," said L. G. Trotter, indicating the fourth button of his waistcoat.

"Tut-tut," said Aunt Dahlia, and I tut-tutted, too, but nobody else expressed the sympathy the writhing man had a right to expect. Florence was still drinking in Percy with every eye at her disposal, and Percy was bending solicitously over Ma Trotter, who was sitting looking like a toad beneath the harrow.

"Come, Moth-aw," said Percy, hoiking her up from where she roosted. "I will bathe your temples with eau-de-Cologne."

With a reproachful look at L. G. Trotter he led her gently from the room. A mother's best friend is her boy.

Aunt Dahlia was still looking aghast, and I knew what was in her mind. Once let this Trotter get away to Liverpool and she would be dished. Delicate negotiations like selling a weekly paper for the gentler sex to a customer full of sales resistance can't be conducted successfully by mail. You have to have men like L. G. Trotter on the spot, kneading their arms and generally giving them the old personality.

"Jeeves!" I cried. I don't know why, because I couldn't see what he could do to help.

He sprang respectfully to life. During the late give-and-take he had been standing in the background with that detached, stuffed-frog look on his face which it always wears when he is present at a free-for-all in which his sense of what is fitting does not allow him to take part. And the spirits rose as I saw from his eye that he was going to rally round.

"If I might make a suggestion, sir."

"Yes, Jeeves?"

"It occurs to me that one of those morning mixtures of mine would bring relief to Mr. Trotter."

I gargled. I got his meaning.

"You mean those pick-me-ups you occasionally prepare for me when the state of the old head seems to call for it?"

"Precisely, sir."

"Would they hit the trot with Mr. Spotter, or rather the other way round?"

"Oh, yes, sir. They act directly on the internal organs."

It was enough. I saw that, as always, he had *tetigisti*-ed the *rem.* I turned to L. G. Trotter.

"You heard?"

"No, I didn't. How do you expect me to hear things—?"

I checked him with one of my gestures.

"Well, listen now," I said. "Be of good cheer, L. G. Trotter, for the United States Marines have arrived. No need for any doctors. Go along with Jeeves, and he will mix you a mixture which will put the old tum in mid-season form before you can say 'Lemuel Gengulphus.'"

He looked at Jeeves with a wild surmise. I heard Aunt Dahlia gasp a gasp.

"Is that right?"

"Yes, sir. I can guarantee the efficacy of the preparation."

L. G. Trotter emitted a loud "Woof!"

"Let's go," he said briefly.

"I'll come with you and hold your hand," said Aunt Dahlia.

"Just one word," I said, as the procession started to file out. "On swallowing the stuff you will have the momentary illusion that you have been struck by lightning. Pay no attention. It's all part of the treatment. But watch the eyeballs, as they are liable, unless checked, to start from the parent sockets and rebound from the opposite wall."

They passed from the room, and I was alone with Florence.

22

IT'S AN ODD THING, but it hadn't occurred to me in the rush and swirl of recent events that, with people drifting off in twos and threes and—in the case of Spode—in ones, the time must inevitably come when this beasel and I would be left face to face in what is called a *solitude à deux*. And now that this unpleasant state of affairs had come about, it was difficult to know how to start the conversation. However, I had a pop at it, the same pop I had had when finding myself closeted with L. G. Trotter.

"Can I get you a sausage?" I said.

She waved it away. It was plain that the unrest in her soul could not be lulled with sausages.

"Oh, Bertie," she said, and paused.

"Or a slice of ham?"

She shook her head. Ham appeared to be just as much a drug in the market as sausages.

"Oh, Bertie," she said again.

"Right opposite you," I said encouragingly.

"Bertie, I don't know what to do."

She signed off once more, and I stood there waiting for something to emerge. A half-formed idea of offering her a kipper I dismissed. Too silly, I mean, keeping on suggesting items on the menu like a waiter trying to help a customer make up his mind.

"I feel awful!" she said.

"You look fine," I assured her, but she dismissed the pretty compliment with another wave of the hand.

She was silent again for a moment, and then it came out with a rush.

"It's about Percy."

I was nibbling a slice of toast as she spoke, but lowered it courteously.

"Percy?" I said.

"Oh, Bertie," she proceeded, and from the way her nose wiggled I could see that she was in quite a state. "All that that happened just now . . . when he said that about not disappointing the woman he loved . . . when I realized what he had done . . . just for me . . ."

"I know what you mean," I said. "Very white."

"Something happened to me. It was as though for the first time I was seeing the real Percy. I had always admired his intellect, of course, but now it was different. I seemed to be gazing into his naked soul, and what I saw there . . ."

"Pretty good, was it?" I queried, helping the thing along.

She drew a deep breath.

"I was overcome. I was stunned. I realized that he was just like Rollo Beaminster."

For a moment I was not abreast. Then I remembered.

"Oh, ah, yes. You didn't get around to telling me much about Rollo, except that he was in wild mood."

"Oh, that was quite early in the story, before he and Sylvia came together again."

"They came together, did they?"

"Yes. She gazed into his naked soul and knew that there could be no other man for her."

I have already stressed the fact that I was mentally at my brightest this morning, and hearing these words I got the distinct idea that she was feeling pretty pro-Percy as of even date. I might be wrong, of course, I didn't think so, and it seemed to me that this was a good thing that wanted pushing along. There is, as Jeeves had so neatly put it, a tide in the affairs of men which, taken at the flood, leads on to fortune.

"I say," I said, "here's a thought. Why don't you marry Percy?"

She started. I saw that she was trembling. She moved, she stirred, she seemed to feel the rush of life along her keel. In her eyes, as she gazed at me, it wasn't difficult to spot the light of hope.

"But I'm engaged to you," she faltered, rather giving the impression that she could have kicked herself for being such a chump.

"Oh, that can be readily adjusted," I said heartily. "Call it off, is my advice. You don't want a weedy butterfly like me about the home, you want something more in the nature of a soulmate, a chap with a number nine hat you can sit and hold hands and talk about T. S. Eliot with. And Percy fills the bill."

She choked a bit. The light of hope was now very pronounced.

"Bertie! You will release me?"

"Certainly, certainly. Frightful wrench, of course, and all that sort of thing, but consider it done."

"Oh, Bertie!"

She flung herself upon me and kissed me. Unpleasant,

of course, but these things have to be faced. As I once heard Anatole remark, one must learn to take a few roughs with a smooth.

We were still linked together in a close embrace, when the silence—we were embracing fairly silently—was broken by what sounded like the heart-cry of one of the local dogs which had bumped its nose against the leg of the table.

It wasn't a dog. It was Percy. He was standing there looking overwrought, and I didn't blame him. Agony, of course, if you love a girl, to come into a room and find her all tangled up with another fellow.

He pulled himself together with a powerful effort.

"Go on," he said, "go on. I'm sorry I interrupted you."

He broke off with a choking gulp, and I could see it was quite a surprise to him when Florence, abruptly detaching herself from me, did a jack rabbit leap that was almost in the Cheesewright-Wooster class and hurled herself into his arms.

"Eh, what?" he said, plainly missing the gist.

"I love you, Percy!"

"You do?" His face lit up for an instant. Then there was a blackout. "But you're engaged to Wooster," he said moodily, eyeing me in a manner that seemed to suggest that in his opinion it was fellows like me who caused half the trouble in the world.

I moved over to the table and took another slice of toast. Cold, of course, but I rather like cold toast, provided there's plenty of butter.

"No, that's off," I said. "Carry on, old sport. You have the green light."

Florence's voice shook.

"Bertie has released me, Percy. I was kissing him because I was so grateful. When I told him I loved you, he released me."

You could see that Percy was impressed.

"I say! That was very decent of him."

"He's like that. Bertie is the soul of chivalry."

"He certainly is. I'm amazed. Nobody would think it, to look at him."

I was getting about fed up with people saying nobody would think it, to look at me, and it is quite possible that I might at this point have said something a bit biting . . . I don't know what, but something. But before I could assemble the makings Florence suddenly uttered something that was virtually tantamount to a wail of anguish.

"But, Percy, what are we to do? I've only a small dress allowance."

I didn't follow the trend of her thought. Nor did Percy. Cryptic, I considered it, and I could see he thought so, too.

"What's that got to do with it?" he said.

Florence wrung her hands, a thing I've often heard about but never seen done. It's a sort of circular movement, starting from the wrists.

"I mean, I haven't any money and you haven't any money, except what your stepfather is going to pay you when you join the business. We should have to live in Liverpool. I can't live in Liverpool!"

Well, of course, lots of people do, or so I have been given to understand, but I saw what she meant. Her heart was in London's Bohemia, Bloomsbury, Chelsea, sandwiches and absinthe in the old studio, all that sort of thing, and she hated to give it up. I don't suppose they have studios up Liverpool way.

"M-m-yes," said Percy.

"You see what I mean?"

"Oh, quite," said Percy.

He was plainly ill at ease. A strange light had come into his tortoiseshell-rimmed spectacles, and his whiskers quivered gently. For a moment he stood there letting "I dare not" wait upon "I would." Then he spoke.

"Florence, I have a confession to make. I hardly know how to tell you. The truth is that my financial position is reasonably sound. I am not a rich man, but I have a satisfactory income, quite large enough to support the home. I have no intention of going to Liverpool."

Florence goggled. I have an idea that she was thinking, early though it was, that he had had one over the eight. Her air was that of a girl on the point of asking him to say "Theodore Oswaldtwistle, the thistle sifter, in sifting a sack of thistles thrust three thorns through the thick of his thumb." However, all she said was:

"But, Percy darling, you surely can't make much out of your poetry?"

He twiddled his fingers for a moment. You could see he was trying to nerve himself to reveal something he would much have preferred to keep under his hat. I have had the same experience when had up on the carpet by my Aunt Agatha.

"I don't," he said. "I only got fifteen shillings for that 'Caliban at Sunset' thing of mine in *Parnassus*, and I had to fight like a tiger to get that. The editress wanted to beat me down to twelve-and-six. But I have a . . . an alternative source of revenue."

"I don't understand."

He bowed his head.

"You will. My receipts from this—er—alternative

source of revenue amounted last year to nearly eight hundred pounds, and this year it should be double that, for my agent has succeeded in establishing me in the American market. Florence, you will shrink from me, but I have to tell you. I write detective stories under the pseudonym of Rex West."

I wasn't looking at Florence, so I don't know if she shrank from him, but I certainly didn't. I stared at him, agog.

"Rex West? Lord-love-a-duck! Did you write *The Mystery of the Pink Crayfish*?" I gasped.

He bowed his head again.

"I did. And *Murder in Mauve, The Case of the Poisoned Doughnut,* and *Inspector Biffen Views the Body.*"

I hadn't happened to get hold of those, but I assured him that I would lose no time in putting them on my library list, and went on to ask a question which had been occupying my mind for quite awhile.

"Then who was it who bumped off Sir Eustace Willoughby, Bart., with the blunt instrument?"

In a low, toneless voice he said:

"Burwash, the butler."

I uttered a cry.

"As I suspected! As I suspected from the first!"

I would have probed further into this Art of his, asking him how he thought up these things and did he work regular hours or wait for inspiration, but Florence had taken the floor again. So far from shrinking from him, she was nestling in his arms and covering his face with burning kisses.

"Percy!" She was all over the blighter. "I think it's wonderful! How frightfully clever of you!"

He tottered.

"You aren't revolted?"

"Of course I'm not. I'm tremendously pleased. Are you working on something now?"

"A novelette. I think of calling it *Blood Will Tell.* It will run to about thirty thousand words. My agent says these American magazines like what they call one-shotters—a colloquial expression, I imagine, for material of a length suitable for publication in a single issue."

"You must tell me all about it," said Florence, taking his arm and heading for the french window.

"Hey, just a moment," I said.

"Yes?" said Percy, turning. "What is it, Wooster? Talk quickly. I am busy."

"May I have your autograph?"

He beamed.

"You really want it?"

"I am a great admirer of your work."

"That is the boy!" said Percy.

He wrote it on the back of an envelope, and they went out hand in hand, those two young folks starting on the long journey together. And I, feeling a bit peckish after this emotional scene, sat down and had another go at the sausages and bacon.

I was still thus engaged when the door opened and Aunt Dahlia came in. A glance was enough to tell me that all was well with the aged relative. On a previous occasion I have described her face as shining like the seat of a bus-driver's trousers. It was doing so now. If she had been going to be Queen of the May, she could not have looked chirpier.

"Has L. G. Trotter signed the papers?" I asked.

"He's going to, the moment he gets his eyeballs back. How right you were about his eyeballs. When last seen,

P. G. WODEHOUSE

they were ricocheting from wall to wall, with him in hot pursuit. Bertie," said the old ancestor, speaking in an awed voice, "what does Jeeves put into those mixtures of his?"

I shook my head.

"Only he and his God know that," I said gravely.

"They seem powerful stuff. I remember reading somewhere once about a dog that swallowed a bottle of tabasco sauce. It was described as putting up quite a performance. Trotter reacted in a somewhat similar manner. I should imagine dynamite was one of the ingredients."

"Very possibly," I said. "But let us not talk of dogs and tabasco sauce. Let us rather discuss these happy endings of ours."

"Endings? In the plural? I've had a happy ending, all right, but you—"

"Me, too. Florence—"

"You don't mean it's off?"

"She's going to marry Percy."

"Bertie, my beamish boy!"

"Didn't I tell you I had faith in my star? The moral of the whole thing, as I see it, is that you can't keep a good man down, or . . ." I bowed slightly in her direction . . . "a good woman. What a lesson this should be to us, old flesh and blood, never to give up, never to despair. However dark the outlook . . ."

I was about to add "and however black the clouds" and go on to speak of the sun sooner or later smiling through, but at this moment Jeeves shimmered in.

"Excuse me, madam. Would it be convenient for you to join Mr. Trotter in the library, madam? He is waiting for you there."

Aunt Dahlia really needs a horse to help her get up

238

speed, but though afoot she made excellent time to the door.

"How is he?" she asked, turning on the threshold.

"Completely restored to health, madam, I am happy to say. He speaks of venturing on a sandwich and a glass of milk at the conclusion of your conference."

She gave him a long, reverent look.

"Jeeves," she said, "you stand alone. I knew you would save the day."

"Thank you very much, madam."

"Have you ever tried those mixtures of yours on a corpse?"

"Not yet, madam."

"You should," said the old relative, and curvetted out like one of those mettlesome steeds which, though I have never heard one do it myself, say "Ha!" among the trumpets.

A silence followed her departure, for I was plunged in thought. I was debating within myself whether to take a step of major importance or whether, on the other hand, not to, and at such times one does not talk, one weighs the pros and cons. I was, in short, standing at a man's crossroads.

That moustache of mine . . .

Pro: I loved the little thing. I fancied myself in it. I had hoped to nurse it through the years with top dressing till it became the talk of the town.

Con: But was it, I asked myself, *safe*? Recalling the effect of its impact on Florence Craye, I saw clearly that it had made me too fascinating. There peril lurked. When you become too fascinating, all sorts of things are liable to occur which you don't want to occur, if you follow me.

A strange calm descended on me. I had made my decision.

"Jeeves," I said, and if I felt the passing pang, why not? One is but human. "Jeeves," I said, "I'm going to shave my moustache."

His left eyebrow flickered, showing how deeply the words had moved him.

"Indeed, sir?"

"Yes, you have earned this sacrifice. When I have eaten my fill . . . Good sausages, these."

"Yes, sir."

"Made, no doubt, from contented pigs. Did you have some for your breakfast?"

"Yes, sir."

"Well, as I was saying, when I have eaten my fill, I shall proceed upstairs to my room, I shall lather the upper lip, I shall take razor in hand . . . and *voilà!*"

"Thank you very much, sir," he said.

Printed in the United States
By Bookmasters